PARA MI FAMILIA DE COCHAMÓ

DAMMED IF YOU DON'T

Chris Kalman

Dammed If You Don't

Cover Design: Sarah Nicholson
Interior Illustrations: Craig Muderlak

Library of Congress Control Number: 2021900702

CPSIA Code: PBANG0518A
ISBN-13: 978-0-578-84097-0

Printed in the United States

ACKNOWLEDGMENTS

Writing a book is hard. It's hard the first time, and as I discovered while writing this story, it can be even harder the second time. If there's one thing I've learned in life, it's that you don't achieve anything hard on your own. Any time you manage to pull off something difficult, even if at times you felt quite alone, thanks are always in order. And so here they are: all my thank-yous, front and center, where they belong.

First, my deep appreciation and gratitude to everyone who supported my Kickstarter. I can't believe how many of you showed up and threw down. The book you're holding in your hands truly would not exist without the Kickstarter backers: especially Justin and Erin Loyka, Darby Rose, Daniel Nethercott, David Wilkinson, Taj and Hollie Vaccarella-Villa, Greg and Alice Greenwood, Muriel Siadak, Jill Ryan, Alex Wildman, Jessica Røki Kilroy, Matt Raue, Lynn and Dawn Studer, Collin Tharp,

Nate Ayers, and Carl Richards—who all contributed particularly heavy lifts.

I technically owe my parents—Dan and Linda Kalman—a thank-you, as they were generous backers too. But of course, I'd be thanking them anyway. I owe my life to them. Not just in the literal "you made me and carried me inside you for nine months and wiped my butt" kind of way, but also in the "you've always been there for me and worked your asses off to give me a good life" kind of way. Not everyone has great parents. I'm forever grateful that I do.

Thank you to everyone who read early drafts of this book and offered me much-needed feedback, advice, and blurbs. Bernadette McDonald, Matt Samet, Brendan Leonard, and Matt Skenazy—thank you. Your expertise and insight are invaluable.

A special thank-you is in order to Craig Childs, who convinced me to throw out an early draft with little promise and start from scratch, working with me on the sentence level to inject some much-needed poesy into the prose; to David Stevenson, who told me the truth when I needed to hear it and advised me to "give the project as much as you possibly can—you'll never regret putting more into it"; and to Kelly Cordes, Derek Franz, and Megan

Kelly, who gave me patient and clearheaded counsel at the very end, helping me make those tiny last-minute changes that make all the difference between a book I'm okay with and a book I'm deeply proud of.

There are three editors I'd like to highlight as well. First, my dear friend and trusted confidant Aaron Mike, who took on the incredibly important task of providing insight into this story from a Native American perspective. Aaron's feedback made this a better, more thoughtful, more equitable, and inclusive book. Second, my partner in crime and fellow Friends of Cochamó board member, Daniel Pastene. Daniel applied his expertise in Chilean slang (both of the arriero and Santiaguino variety) to the dialogue and helped make it as authentic as possible. Muchisimas gracias, hueón. Finally, to Lindsey Nelson, who took on the daunting task of copy editing all my crappy grammar and punctuation. This book would be an absolute mess without you.

Thank you to Sarah Nicholson for doing such an incredible job with the cover design and helping me lay out the book for printing. And a huge thank you to Craig Muderlak for not only creating five original illustrations in a completely new and unique style but also for all his help with prints and promoting the Kickstarter.

Thank you to my fiancée, Megan Kelly, who kept pushing and pushing me to let her read this before it was out in print and then proved to be an indispensable editor and sounding board when I finally caved. Also for being my life partner, best friend, and occasional therapist.

Finally, I want to thank my entire Cochamó family: Grant Simmons, without whom I never would have gone in the first place. JB Haab who took me under his wing and taught me to fly with the condors. Daniel Seeliger, Silvina Verdún, and Zenon, who always made me feel like family and are an endless source of inspiration. Nahir, my Argentinean sister. Mono, my Mapuche brother. Favián, Tati, and all the Sandovals, who are some of the first people I think of when I think of the reasons to protect Cochamó. Chris, Cooper, Austin, Flo, Miranda, Dustin, Zdzislaw, Nico, Eric, Kirk, Chance, Chip, and everyone else I've had the privilege to put up new routes or tie in with in Cochamó. Thank you to Jupi, Martu, Pato, Moni, Ailén, Pauli, Juan, Sofia, Turco, Flor, Rudy (do Brasil), Rudy (de Cochamó), José, Josefina, Trevor, Nelson, Neha, Vianney, Pauline, Chiquiño, Elsa, Mike, Patricio, Cochela, Cochelo, Lechero, Horacio, Andrés, Paolo, Christian, Jorjato, Don Claudio, and all the rest who have always made my time in Cochamó so special. And to Organización Valle Cochamó, Puelo Patagonia, Puelo Sin Torres, my colleagues at Friends of Cochamó, and all the people in the world fighting to protect the greater Cochamó area…thank you. I owe you a debt of gratitude. We all do.

CHAPTER I

THEY SET OUT AT DAWN from the little fishing village of Calihue. Cocksure roosters strutted and crowed along the margins of the sole road in and out of town. Rotund pigs rooted indolently through the soft summer soil in the grassy yards of ramshackle houses. The Coinco fjord lapped gently at its shores as mist rose from the water in thin sheets, like so many spirits summoned upward by the rising sun.

It was Christmas Eve, 2011. Nahuel—the only rider native to the region, the other two being gringos from *el norte*—thought it ominous to work on the auspicious day. But they paid good wages. Moreover, Nahuel's curiosity had gotten the better of him. The gringos came to climb huge walls of stone, so they said. But surely there must be rocks where they came from; otherwise, how would they know how to climb? There had to be some other reason for their sudden appearance way down south in Chilean Patagonia. *Oro quizás*, Nahuel thought, having heard rumor before that the mountains of his home were filled with gold. He lashed the loads down tight and fastened the saddles.

Across the fjord, great mountains sprawled into the distance—their tops bare, grayly granitic, and shrouded in mist. They traversed a two-track etched into a cut bank—the Río Lahuenco clear and emeraldine below. The brackish estuary where the river met the fjord soon gave way to dense, dark coastal rain forest. Mud sucked at the horses' hooves as the riders ducked low-slung branches that hung over the trail. Everything was green. Green lichen, green moss, green shafts of light filtered through the green canopy of leaves. The color palette reminded John and Gary of their home in the Pacific Northwest, but the bird calls were foreign, the smells unfamiliar, and the trail unlike any they had ever seen. Steep walls rose on either side of them like a slot canyon, but the walls were made of mud. At times the corridor was so narrow the horses could not turn around. But they did not need to, for Nahuel was an expert horseman and guided the horses assiduously.

After three hours of tough riding, the forest canopy finally parted, and unfettered sunlight poured down upon them. Massive monoliths of vertical white granite, previously hidden by the dense woods, suddenly appeared. Gary dismounted clumsily, falling to his knees like a pilgrim and gazing upon the bleached pinnacles. John bore a peculiar look of self-satisfaction, as if he had known all his life he would one day arrive at such a place. He and Nahuel stepped down from their mounts and joined Gary for a much-needed break and lunch. Nahuel made sandwiches of *pancito*—flat, round rolls of white bread—filled with avocado, tomato, cheese, and salami. They ate hungrily. When they had finished, John pulled out a celebratory bottle of whiskey and tilted it toward Gary, smirking, as if to say *I told you so*. Gary declined, feeling John always celebrated too early. But Nahuel asked, "*¿Porque no?*" his eyes twinkling. So John uncorked the bottle and passed it to Nahuel, who took a long pull. Then John drank and put the bottle away. "*Vale*," Nahuel said, "*vámonos*," and they loaded up and set off into the forest again.

After another hour of riding, they came upon a bucolic meadow of tall green grass. A narrow windrow of trees stretched along the banks of the Lahuenco, which oxbowed and goosenecked around white beaches—some of fine sand and some of boulders the size, shape, and texture of bowling balls. On the other side of the river, the forest rose steeply. The green tapestry was unbroken but for occasional small rips, where gleaming waterfalls or steep escarpments of black rock poked through. Above the forest stood the great peaks they had seen before, looking now like an upturned rib cage or the teeth of some snarling beast. John took out a worn leather notebook and began jotting notes for the article he was planning to write about the wall he was planning to climb, as if the deed were already done. He put down the notebook and glassed the walls with binoculars, swatting at the *tábanos*—horseflies—that swarmed around his face. Gary declined the binoculars when John offered. He was happy enough to look upon the world with the naked eye, reclining in the grass, soaking in the sunshine.

Nahuel unloaded the animals and set them to graze in the pasture. He eyed the large expedition duffels emblazoned with the logos of the gringos' sponsors curiously, wondering what esoteric and expensive paraphernalia they must contain. John and Gary ended their reverie, pitching tents and tarps for makeshift rain shelters while Nahuel built a fire and filled two five-gallon buckets with water from the river. They cooked rice, beans, and fillets of Nahuel's freshly caught salmon over the open flame. After dinner and a cursory rinse of the dishes, John and Gary retired to their tents. Nahuel laid out his bedroll beneath a blanket of stars, failing to comprehend the gringos' choice to sleep beneath plastic roofs as he stared at the dazzling cosmos. But there was much about the gringos he did not understand.

NAHUEL WOKE TO BIRDSONG BEFORE the sunrise, a light mist blanketing the valley floor. He stood up sleepily to relieve himself, nearly pissing on his feet when John clapped him on the back with a boisterous, "Buenos días, amigo!" The gringos were already up, sorting climbing gear, food, a sleeping bag, and a first aid kit into piles on a blue tarp between the tents. Nahuel rubbed his eyes, muttering something under his breath about it being Christmas morning, *hueones culiaos*.

"*¿Quieren desayunar?*" Nahuel asked, hoping they might stay for breakfast.

Gary held out what looked like a turd in a

foil wrapper, laughing at Nahuel's unrestrained look of disgust at the energy bar. Gary and John shouldered their bags, grabbed machetes, and began walking matter-of-factly toward the river. Nahuel raised an eyebrow and asked where they were going.

"*Allá*," John said, pointing at the tallest cliff on the south side of the river.

"*Conchetumare*," Nahuel whispered, looking up at the peak.

"We come back mañana," John said in his broken Spanish, "*o día después.*"

"*Bueno, que les vaya bien.*"

John and Gary cut poles of *caña colihue*—an austral relative of the bamboo family—and awkwardly staggered their way across the river. The water did not rise above their hips, but the current was strong, and the bed was lined with slippery round stones, which shifted under their bare feet. They waved to Nahuel after making it to the other side and lacing up shoes, then disappeared into the forest.

They macheted their way straight up the mountain slope, climbing the springy branches of *lenga* where the terrain was near vertical. The steep climb gave way to a somber and quiet plateau where three-thousand-year-old alerce trees stood tall and stoic as redwoods. After three hours of hard and sweaty hiking, they were finally at the toe of the buttress. The wall seemed to curve like a scythe or a crescent moon—slabby at first, then vertical, and finally overhung, the top guarded by roofs and hanging bottomless corners.

They walked along the base of the wall searching for weaknesses in the fortress of stone—a crack system that went from bottom to top or a series of corners connected by narrow fissures. Anything but blank, mirror-smooth swaths of vertical rock. Here, Gary did take the binoculars and used them to investigate microfeatures far up the thousand-meter wall.

"There," he said. "You see?"

John took the binos and nodded. "What about the roof at the top?" he asked.

"What about it?" Gary grinned. He loved overhangs, as John well knew. John rolled his eyes and sighed. Gary's intuition was probably right. He always seemed to find a way.

They set down their packs and took a brief break, setting their sweat-soaked shirts to dry on the sunny slab. But neither one could sit still, both nervous and excited as they were. Out from the packs came the gear. On went the harnesses. They rock paper scissored to see who would go first.

Gary won, so he tied in to the top side of the rope (John, the bottom), changed into climbing shoes, and clipped aluminum chocks and spring-loaded camming devices to his harness. He and John bumped fists, their spirits flying like school children at recess. Then he began to climb.

Gary was mesmerizing as he moved up the wall—all controlled strength and elegant balance. He pressed the flat soles of his shoes into the granite like a gecko, adhering through unseen forces. He did not pull his body up with his arms but used his palms to shift his center of gravity left and right above his feet, allowing his leg muscles to generate the upward momentum. He was neither quick nor slow; his body neither rigid nor flaccid. He flowed like water in reverse. As Gary climbed, John fed rope through his belay device, giving just enough slack not to restrict Gary's movement but not so much as to unnecessarily lengthen a potential fall. At one hundred feet, John called out, "Half rope," letting Gary know that in another hundred feet there would be no more rope to give. Gary climbed fifty feet farther until he reached a flat ledge the size of a park bench. He stopped, built an anchor, clipped in, and yelled down, "Off belay!"

They climbed in a way that resembled a long and drawn-out game of hopscotch. Gary would climb up, pause at a stance to build an anchor, and John would follow. Then John would lead to a logical stopping point, build an anchor, and Gary would follow. They would not have seemed—had they been watched through a spotting scope as is done in the Alps—to move quickly. Nor did they tarry, except for sections where the crack was swallowed by mud and vegetation, forcing them to pause at tenuous stances and scrape desperately with fingernails and wire brushes to excavate a spot to place protection. When these efforts were fruitless, they gathered courage and continued climbing unprotected, hoping to find better luck ahead. Both climbers were fortunate on multiple occasions to avoid potentially fatal falls. They climbed through the day, the meters and hours falling steadily away behind them.

Just below the summit, the wall jutted overhead like the prow of a ship—a difficult and ominous ending to an already-challenging climb. It was John's turn to lead. He looked up with fear in his heart, not perceiving any possible way to surmount the overhanging wall. He took the rack and attempted to traverse left instead but was quickly dead-ended at a blank expanse. He came back to Gary, shrugged, then tried to circumvent the prow to the right.

As Gary belayed these efforts, he looked up at the seemingly impossible overhang. A series of aberrations in the smooth surface of the stone presented themselves as possible hand and footholds, and his mind organized these holds into a meaningful pattern, just as the stargazer forms a constellation out of the chaos of stars. He imagined his body executing an elaborate dance: left hand up to the inverted undercling, right hand far right to the vertical edge, left heel pressed onto the protruding knob, right toe pushing down on the small nub of quartz, left hand up to the hand crack. Then the hard part: spin the body 180 degrees and kick the feet upside down over the head, catching the lip of the roof with the toes. Place protection in the hand crack. Right hand to the lip, then left hand. Spin back around. Press down. Belly up onto the ledge. He could feel his pectoral muscles flexing through the compression moves, the calf muscle burning from the heel hook, the vertiginous feeling of inverting with one thousand meters of air sprawled out beneath him.

John made his way back to the anchor, looking defeated and talking about going down. But Gary interrupted him and walked him through the sequence he had envisioned.

"I told you we should have brought the bolts,"

John said. If they had, they could have safely protected the path Gary suggested.

"I don't need the bolts," Gary said. "Give me the rack."

John shook his head but did as he was told. Then he belayed, watching dumbfounded and awestruck as Gary flawlessly climbed the moves exactly as he had described them—the veins bulging in his forearms, his breathing deep and intentional as he maintained composure through the dangerous inversion. He disappeared over the lip of the roof, then let out a victorious whoop, which rang through the valley.

Gary pulled up the slack and put John on belay. Then John tried the moves. He made it to the inversion by the skin of his teeth but lacked the abdominal strength to kick his foot over the lip. He fell on the taut rope, swinging into space. *Jesus Christ*, he thought, grateful to be following instead of leading, and trying not to imagine what would have happened to Gary had he been the one to fall instead. Unable to swing back into the wall, John was forced to tie two Prusiks and ascend the rope to Gary.

Now safely on relatively flat ground, they untied, coiled the rope, slung it over a pack, and hiked the last hundred meters of nontechnical ridge to the summit. When they arrived, the light was fading, and everything was cast in a sublime crepuscular stillness. The air chilled; the bellies of clouds shone with the final pink radiance of day; the clicking of bats seeking insects filled the air. Gary was struck by the sensation of being watched by unseen creatures.

To the south, buttress after buttress extended into the distance like layers of an onion, cut in half and left peeling away from each other on the counter. North, on the other side of the Río Lahuenco, alpine ridges emptied their snowfields into sapphire lakes. East, the deep emerald defile and the shimmering river went on as far as the eye could see. Down below was the peaceful meadow at the forest's edge. They could just make out their tents—small dots of out-of-place fluorescence on the grassy ground. And to the west, a blood orange sun melted into the Coinco fjord. The village of Calihue was somewhere in the distance, along the two-track that wrapped out of sight to the north.

They settled in to sleep upon the summit, which was not—it turned out—a dramatic point at all but a plateau as broad and flat as a football field. They spread out ropes as makeshift pads and huddled together under a single sleeping bag, breathing small clouds into the quickening darkness. The gaseous glow of a thousand galaxies bombarded their tired minds, barring them from sleep. The Southern Cross, the luminous Milky Way, an endless stream of shooting stars. They spent hours in silent wonder at the world they inhabited, their place in it, the inconceivable fact that no other human had ever been in precisely that spot, had ever set foot on that lonesome summit before. Finally they slept.

In the morning, they made their way south to the back of the cirque, opting for a descent through the thronging forest instead of rappelling the face. This proved to be more challenging than anticipated, the path of least resistance being devious with frequent climbs up and down steep ridges. Finally they reached a narrow pass. To the north lay a granite amphitheater split by a sinuous freshet, which disappeared into the steep forest they had climbed the day before, then reappeared where it merged with the Río Lahuenco far below. On the other side of the pass to the south was another valley, deeply carved eons ago by glaciers and filled in now with lagunas and rivers, rain forest and swamps.

They paused on this isthmus of slickrock to eat the last of their food—the least appetizing of their energy bars—before beginning the arduous trek through the jungle back to base camp. The sun was warm, but even the slightest breeze made them shiver in their sweat-drenched shirts. As they stuffed the wrappers from the bars into their rucksacks, John noticed what he thought was a small gray lizard moving slowly across the ground toward them. Except it didn't scurry like a lizard. Rather, it plodded on stubby legs. John bent down to get a closer look and saw that the skin was smooth and rubbery—not scaly—with something of a liquid sheen. He did a double take. The small quadruped wasn't a lizard at all but a salamander.

What business a salamander had on that cold and inhospitable ridge John could not fathom. Furthermore, as he cast back through his memory to a not-brief period of elementary school when he had taken an interest in herpetology, he seemed to recall having read that salamanders did not exist in the southern hemisphere at all, or some such piece of trivia. And yet, there it was—undoubtedly and indisputably a living, breathing salamander. He reached out to coax the slippery creature into his hand, but a shadow fell over him.

"Don't," Gary said with finality.

"But look at it!" John insisted. *It was distinctly cute*, he thought, *even handsome*—its lips curled into a friendly smile, bright bulbous eyes looking in wonder at the wide world.

"Amazing," Gary said, "just one more reason to leave it alone." Gary's was a more detached form of reverence—an unspoken faith in the soundness of the natural world coupled with a justifiable wariness of man's meddling in it. He liked to be "out in nature," as people say, but dissecting it with scalpels, magnifying glasses, and taxonomies always struck him as voyeuristic. Not so John, who had majored in biology as an undergrad.

"Let's go," Gary said as he shouldered his pack and started heading down a steep col into the granite bowl. John frowned, snapped a few pictures of the salamander, and followed Gary down. The going at the start was tenuous—steep, exposed fins of exfoliating granite wet with snowmelt—and required them to do a series of rappels. Then they were in the jungle, and for six sweaty hours they swatted and chopped with machetes through the teeming selva. Eventually they were deposited in a granite-bottomed streambed, which they waded through slowly but gratefully, happy to give the machetes a rest.

NAHUEL WAS LOUNGING BY THE river, lazily sharpening his knife on a round stone when John and Gary returned. He stared in disbelief when they burst through the woods covered in mud and plant debris, soaked to the bone and soiled like hardrock miners, whooping and hollering victoriously. They splashed drunkenly into the river. Halfway across, John slipped and fell in, gasping when he emerged from the frigid water. He laughed at himself heartily, and then they were all laughing, exchanging hugs and exclamations, pointing at the peak and telling the tale in pantomimed Spanglish.

They all went up to camp where Nahuel prepared a maté. As they sipped, John's tireless mind was already scheming.

"*¿Tiene el…pronóstico?*" he asked, consulting his Spanish dictionary for "weather forecast."

"*Sipo*," Nahuel replied, followed by a long string of idioms about various permutations of rain, which John could not decipher. His Spanish was passable, but Nahuel's singsong rhythm and thick accent eluded him.

"*¿Qué?*" he inquired.

Nahuel shrugged, shaking his head.

"*Sol*," he said sarcastically, gesturing toward the sun. "*Puro sol.*"

John looked over toward Gary, who was rifling through the tents for the satellite device to check in with his wife. Then John looked back up at the mountains, linking corners and cracks and other features from bottom to top, plotting out his next climb.

IT HAD BEEN RAINING IN Seattle for weeks and was raining still. Alison Porter watched fat drops splash the sidewalk through the window of her and Gary's Beacon Hill apartment and considered her options. She could bike the eleven-odd miles to the Mercers' home in Bellevue, and ordinarily she would have, rain be damned—you didn't make it in a place like Seattle without a healthy tolerance for precipitation. But if she did bike, she'd have to hire a babysitter, and that was expensive. On the other hand, she could simply drive and drop three-year-old Braden at her parents' house in Columbia City on the way. Which wasn't so bad, really. In the end, she just wished Gary was there. It wasn't that she resented him being gone. She knew how important the expeditions were to him, but the reality of his absence and the chaos it wreaked upon her daily routine grew more burdensome each year—especially now that they had Braden.

Gary had been gone for nearly a month now, and even Alison's deep stores of patience were running low. She didn't want to drive. She didn't want to hire a babysitter. She wanted Gary to take care of his son so she could go for a rainy bike ride, drink wine with her friend, and turn off her brain for a while. She sighed a small cloud of frustration against the windowpane.

Alison eventually decided to drop Braden with her parents. She made the stop, apologizing to her mom in her native tongue, Korean, for leaving so quickly after a single cup of tea, then cursed her way across the Lake Washington bridge, which was already swollen with rush hour traffic. What would have taken five minutes by bike took half an hour by car. *Hashtag progress*, she thought, as human civilization lumbered along slowly toward whatever fate awaited. She finally arrived at Brooke and John's "humble abode," as they called their million-dollar cottage, parked, and sloshed her way to the door. She didn't knock but let herself in as usual.

"Hey!" Brooke called from the kitchen where she was making tea.

"Hey, girl!" Alison called back. There was a fire glowing in the wood stove. Alison grabbed a blanket from the leather couch and curled up on the rug in front of the blaze. Brooke came out moments later and wrapped her arms extravagantly around Alison, hiccupping, evidently already tipsy.

"Fuck men," she said, a wry smile parting her wine-stained lips, and handed a glass to Alison.

"To fucking men," Alison agreed, and they clinked glasses and drank.

It had been over a week since either of them had heard from their spouses. They weren't worried so much as peeved—particularly Brooke who, after all these years with John, knew that any time she gave him an inch he'd take a mile. Brooke had barely sat down before she was regaling Alison with her many frustrations. John could go a year without seeing her and not mind, not even notice. He was so focused on everything else in his life—the climbing, the travel, the photography. She felt she was number four on his list, at best.

"It didn't used to be that way," she said. "I mean, when we met at that slide show—you know, the one at Feathered Friends, way back when—I remember how he looked at me. It was crazy. I never felt that before. It wasn't those stupid fuck-me eyes that gross assholes have been giving me ever since I hit puberty. It was something else. You know? Like, he wanted to be with me. Forever. Like he saw me and instantly knew that I was part of the plan."

Brooke turned from the fire and looked at Alison.

"When I say it out loud, knowing John how he is now, it sounds stupid. But is it?" She asked. "I mean, am I stupid for having believed…having felt…that?"

Alison stopped rubbing Brooke's arm, held her hand, and said, "Hell no, girl. It's not stupid and neither are you. He's changed. One hundred percent."

"You know what I feel like?" Brooke said. "I feel like when you're watching one of those stupid Netflix series, and you don't even like the show anymore, but you keep watching episode after episode because you just have to see how it's going to end. And the worst part is, you already know! Except the thing is, at first, I thought I was a main character. Now I just feel like some vague and replaceable extra. And that pisses me off. I've worked my ass off, studied hard, made opportunities for myself that have nothing to do with John. I'd be fine without him. Maybe even better."

Alison didn't know whether to reassure Brooke about John or encourage her to dump his sorry ass. She had her own misgivings about him, mostly surrounding the effect he had upon Gary. Gary's ambitions were more modest than John's, which suited Alison just fine. He wanted to be a good husband, a good father, a solid climber, and little more. Or so he claimed. But Gary felt small in John's presence, and all of a sudden, he would be plagued by an itch to drop everything and travel the world putting up first ascents. The change of heart was disorienting to Alison, but it was even worse for Gary, who would suddenly find himself questioning everything he and Alison had worked for and built together. Gary loved John—they had been friends and climbing partners since before Alison had entered the picture. But Gary was changing. John was changing. Their relationship was changing. In the past, spending time with John made Gary feel alive. These days it just left him depressed.

Undoubtedly, it was in part due to the photography issue. John's constant obsession with "getting the shot" and asking Gary to pose for pictures had been innocuous enough in the early years of their partnership. But lately, it struck Gary as intrusive, if not exploitative. Back in the day, it had felt like the reason Gary was in the shots was because he was a 5.13 trad climber—no mean feat at the time. But the landscape had changed. Strong trad climbers were a dime a dozen now, but strong *Native American* trad climbers were few and far between. With all of these companies and magazines becoming suddenly interested in diversity, equity, and inclusion, all the opportunities coming Gary's way felt like they had way more to do with his heritage than his climbing acumen. Gary certainly preferred the weird flattery he felt in the climbing ranks to the overt racism of "the real world." But the situation still bothered him. After all, he was only half Native. His father, Jonah—a Skykomish who left the Tulalip Reservation early in life—never spoke about his time on the reservation; he never taught Gary Lushootseed, Chinook, or any other Salish dialect; he never shared the stories of their people. Gary was raised in a mostly white neighborhood with his reticent father and his white mom. He tried in vain to make sense of who and what he was. A white Indian. A brown white guy. He felt unmoored in his own body, and the sound of the shutter on John's camera was a constant reminder of his uncomfortable straddling of disparate worlds.

The two women left their teacups largely untouched, opting instead to finish a bottle of Barbera d'Alba in front of the fire while researching their own climbing trip, a couple months out. But Brooke was too distracted to be of any use.

"City of Rocks might be a perfect destination

in March," Alison suggested.

"I could just break John's knees when he gets back, and then he'd *have* to stay home," Brooke replied.

Alison said nothing, inwardly relieved that she didn't have these problems with Gary; then she thought better of her silence and assured Brooke that John would get it out of his system eventually. Brooke smiled bitterly, knowing it was not true.

They ordered pad thai and tom kha from the local Thai restaurant—the delivery driver *waiing* obsequiously in the pouring rain after Brooke's generous tip—and watched a documentary about Beyoncé while they ate. They were bringing the dishes to the kitchen when their cell phones buzzed in unison. Gary and John had finally been able to get out a message on the satellite phone.

"Great success!" Gary wrote to Alison. "Can't wait to tell you. See you soon (three days)! Love you."

John's message to Brooke read: "First ascent in bag. Good weather coming! Extending trip one week. See you soon."

Alison could discern the contents of John's message by the look on Brooke's face. She gave Brooke a hug and asked whether a baseball bat or a sledgehammer would be a more appropriate tool for John's upcoming operation.

An uncomfortable silence descended, and Alison took the opportunity to excuse herself. It was getting late, and she had to get home to pick up Braden. Brooke nodded, gave her a long hug, and walked her to the door. As she watched Alison disappear into the rain, she silently cursed the soft spot in her heart that sent tears falling down her cheeks.

IN THE MORNING, THE HEAVY fog of hangover erased all memory of the bad dreams Brooke had shuddered through the night before. She forced down fried eggs and a banana—both well-known palliatives for the comeuppance of heavy drink—and by noon she was more or less restored. She thought she'd call David, John's father, then changed her mind. She already knew that he would have precious little to offer in the way of advice. He had no answers for John's impetuousness. John had decided at an early age that he and he alone was in charge of his life. Trying to talk some greater forethought or rounder reckoning into him was like talking to a brick wall, and Brooke could picture David shrugging hopelessly on the other end of the line.

She looked at the framed photograph of the Mercer men that hung in the foyer. There was David, stoic and regal; John, wearing that smirk of derision he brought to all formal affairs; and then there was John's older, more conservative brother, Peter. She toyed momentarily with the notion of calling Peter, with whom she carried on a mostly feigned flirtation, more for the unlikely goal of arousing John's jealousy than any actual interest. But while David would be merely useless, Peter's legitimate resentment would only further frustrate her with John. Peter, like David, had been castigated by John for his participation in the family timber business for far too long. He was weary to the point of tears of John's sanctimonious preaching. Everyone used paper. People wiped their asses with it. The photos John got paid for were printed on it. Peter would have more sympathy for John's tree-hugging rhetoric if he wasn't constantly flying all over the world to climb—an activity as frivolous as it was useless—polluting the atmosphere with God knows how much carbon emissions in the process. Peter might even intimate that perhaps Brooke should consider another Mercer altogether, but that was not a road she intended to go down.

She went through a mental Rolodex of people other than her own girlfriends (for she already knew what they would say) that she could talk to about John. But there was nobody. It dawned on her that Gary was not just John's best, but perhaps his only, friend of any real intimacy. She wondered if Gary knew that. Then she wondered if John knew it. It wasn't that John was a loner. It was something else. He was searching for something. Trying to figure out what on Earth he could care about enough to devote himself to. Family never fit the bill and, these days, neither did Brooke. There was a hole, and he didn't know what to fill it with. So he simply filled it with more of himself.

The problem with John, Brooke had come to learn the hard way, was that so long as he continued moving, he never felt lonely. And he moved all the time. But even John would have sedentary periods—floored by bad weather, work, or other obligations—and that's when the loneliness caught up with him. He would scramble to pick up the pieces of the relationships he'd defaulted on. He would come home, give her more attention, and things would be good for a while. But then, as predictable as the changing of the seasons, he'd grow restless and disappear again. That was the crux of the problem. It wasn't that John didn't want or need human affection. It was that he was caught in a loop, doomed—like Sisyphus—to wage the same futile struggle again and again.

JOHN SAT BENEATH A BLUE tarp in an unending downpour, thinking that perhaps by extending his ticket he had made a mistake. Hadn't Nahuel said *puro sol*? The dirty liar. Now he was alone with the suddenly quiet forest, the dismal sky, and a small bird that kicked and scratched in the food scraps of the firepit, repeating the eponymous call—"wet wet, wet wet"—for which it was named. But the huet-huet also sang another tune—a forlorn and fading decrescendo that implored the listener to "work work work work work work work."

You can't have it both ways, John thought, looking at the raindrops bouncing off the kiddy-pool-sized puddles that had collected in the pampa overnight. Yes, there was work to be done. Endless walls to be climbed. Routes to be named. Trails to be cut. Photographs to be published. Maps to be made. Campgrounds to be built. The place was brimming with potential energy. A veritable Yosemite Valley, but utterly virgin. His brain spun with the possibilities as he thought more about what he might become as the progenitor of those routes, photographs, and campgrounds than the fate of the valley itself. But the rain had him grounded. Wet wet. Nothing could be accomplished until the skies cleared.

"Salamander weather," he said out loud, startling the huet-huet, which cocked its head, looked at him briefly through a white-ringed eye, then resumed its scratching. It acted just like a miniature chicken: pulling the duff and leaf litter backward with outsized feet in long, sweeping motions, then pecking at the exposed earth for whatever tasty detritus had been revealed. John thought back to the unusual salamander he had seen on the summit, comparing and contrasting it in memory to the Mount Lyell salamander which he and Gary had come across in the Sierra Nevada during a ridge traverse two and a half years prior. Gary hadn't cared about that one either. John had always been miffed that Gary didn't seem to have any interest in the Latin names of creatures or to understand precisely how they fit into the complicated tapestry of the larger ecosystem. Gary had no desire to touch or hold things. Nothing seemed to strike him as more or less interesting than anything else. He had no sense of the exotic.

Gary didn't conform with John's notion of what a Native American was supposed to be, or believe, or how one was supposed to behave. But that didn't seem to matter to the publishers and gear companies footing the bills for their trip. Gary was a bona fide Native American, and that was good enough. Perhaps it played in John's favor that Gary's heritage made him a particularly attractive model. *So?* John thought defensively. *What of it?* After all, increasing diversity in the outdoor industry was innately good, not to mention overdue. Should he, John Mercer, feel bad for aiding and abetting that cause? Moreover, the relationship wasn't exactly parasitic. Hadn't Gary benefited from having his photo plastered all over the magazines and the sponsorships that followed? Sure, there were occasional examples of disingenuousness and tokenism. But it was all in the service of a greater good, and if there was one thing John believed in in life, it was that. Human individuals were small, insignificant, and meaningless in the grand scheme of things. No single person's joy or suffering amounted to more than a drop of water in a massive tsunami. John didn't care about individual drops; he was moved by the inertia of the wave itself. Where would the wave crash, and what would be underneath when it did? Those were the questions he was interested in. And while he wasn't a surfer, he had every intention of using his one precious life—to quote Mary Oliver, whose considerable poetic output had been reduced in the popular sphere to little more than an internet meme—to find the biggest wave he could and ride it.

What a stupid idea, John thought. He stood up and walked out from under the trees into the open field. He couldn't even see the damn mountains the cloud cover was so thick. *Waves*, he thought, as he watched wave after wave of rain blow through. All of it was stupid, and he was stupid for thinking it. He missed Brooke. He knew the second Gary and Nahuel rode off into the forest that he had made a mistake, but he had been too stubborn to admit it then, and it was too late to fix it now. He imagined Gary tearing up at corny movies on the flight. Imagined Brooke and Alison coming to meet them at the airport. Imagined Brooke's warm lips, the curve of her butt, her hands upon him, that look in her eyes. Then the vision disappeared into the rain and the gray. He looked at his watch, decided four o'clock was late enough to start drinking, and uncorked a bottle of whiskey. "To the sun," he said to no one in particular, tossing one back. He was passed out by eight.

As if John's words had been prophetic, he did wake to sunlight. The rain-washed mountains were gleaming in the dawn, and John immediately forgot about the revelations of yesterday: about Brooke, Gary, and all the other humans on the planet, the majority of whom he thought were slovenly and hardly worth the oxygen they consumed. He hastily packed a bag with too much of what he didn't need (warm clothing, as the sunlight quickly transformed the rain forest from temperate to tropical), and not enough of what he did need (gear to safely protect the climb), and set off. This time, he set his sights on a tall peak on the same side of the river as camp. Again, he macheted his way through the forest, charting a stubbornly direct course for the mountain's mostly forested, yet still precipitously steep, south shoulder. The terrain mostly consisted of absurdly steep hiking and Tarzanesque tree climbing. The going was tough and often scary. He never stopped smiling.

Twelve hours later, he stood on the summit. He named the peak Cerro Nahuel for his new friend and for the tracks he had seen in the mud during the approach to the wall—Nahuel meaning "puma" in Mapudungun, the tongue of the Mapuche people native to the region. He gazed in awe at the cirque across the Río Lahuenco, crowned by

Cerro Salamandra, as he and Gary had dubbed the imposing peak they climbed. High above, he saw condors gliding toward unseen goals. *Here*, he thought, *is something good*. Not a power line, satellite tower, road, house, car, parking lot, gift shop, or any other of mankind's adulterations in sight. Pure and pristine wilderness. Perfection incarnate.

"You cannot improve upon it," he remembered Theodore Roosevelt saying about the Grand Canyon. "The ages have been at work on it, and man can only mar it."

But he did not recall that other famous Roosevelt quote. "I don't go so far as to think that the only good Indian is the dead Indian, but I believe nine out of every ten are, and I shouldn't like to inquire too closely into the case of the tenth."

Like many white men before him, John Mercer's ideal of wilderness as something outside of and separate from humans was couched in racism. The notion that "man can only mar it" was not only a dismissal of the indigenous people who had sustainably coexisted with and lived in the Grand Canyon and other ecosystems for thousands of years—it was a prescription for their removal.

CHAPTER II

What does it mean to die anyway?

That is what David Mercer wondered as he stared out the window at the insipid Seattle sky. What happens to the body, he understood. But the energy that animates the cells, the thoughts and emotions that fill the skull—what happens to all of that?

His vision peeled back from the gray clouds of the outside world, came in through the window, and returned to his eyelids, which closed now against Peter's yammering on the phone. He wished he had lids for his ears. "Where the hell is John?" Peter demanded of whatever poor soul was on the other side of the call. He had been asking everyone he talked to over the last hour. David had the same question but for different reasons. While

Peter was filled with indignation, David was simply curious. What grand adventure was John on now?

David had been the picture of good health for a sixty-four-year-old male. A less fit man might have been spared by earlier detection, but his robustness had masked the symptoms of the cancer, and the disease had metastasized from his lungs to his lymphatic system and up to his brain. The doctors gave him six months to live with chemo and radiation, an unknowably shorter duration if he eschewed the recommended treatments. He elected the latter—having witnessed the horrors of traditional oncology during his own father's battle with cancer—and began to put his affairs in order.

His chief concern in the final months of his life was how to divvy up the massive Mercer fortune. There was a case to be made for leaving the lion's share to Peter. After all, Peter had been far more present in David's life since the diagnosis, not to mention over the past couple decades. Moreover, Peter had followed in David's footsteps, while John had snubbed and scorned his father's path. But since the chilling news three months earlier, the moribund man had begun to reflect on the brevity of life and how much of it he had wasted. It occurred to him for the first time that perhaps there was something recommendable to John's restlessness—his quest for something more meaningful than a paycheck and a pension. Where he had once thought of John as his biggest failure, he now began to think that it had been he and Peter who had failed to do something useful with their time on Earth.

The shift in perspective felt like a sea change to David. And yet, it was not entirely unprecedented. Hadn't he always envied John's nonteleological, almost Taoist, approach to life? Especially after the pointless and tragic death of Sara—David's wife—at the hands of some idiot drunk driver. In the aftermath of Sara's death, David had begun thinking that he would like to spend his retirement joining John on some of his adventures. He never divulged this to John but made sure to pay him enough favors (usually financial) to guilt him into acquiescence if and when the time for such a request ever came. Now that he was dying, those plans were shot. He did not curse God nor fear his fate. But the imminence of his early departure from this world further convinced him that John had seen quite clearly what he and Peter had missed—that life was for living, not saving up for tomorrow.

Peter finally shut up, hugged David, and left him in the hospital room in relative peace. David returned to gazing through the rain-streaked windows, searching for signs of life. A crow, a raven, a gyre of buzzards on the wing. A wayward butterfly drifted past. Curious. How did that old story John liked go again? Something about "Am I a butterfly dreaming I'm Chuang Tzu, or am I Chuang Tzu dreaming I'm a butterfly?"

David made, in that moment, one of the most impulsive decisions of his life. He resolved to leave the majority of the inheritance to John. Could he really be so bold, even reckless? It was no small sum: more than $30 million—the accrued wealth of four generations of hardworking Mercers. Well, why not? The old guard was gone now. Just he and the boys—soon to be just the boys—remained. And when it came to them, the more he thought about it, the more sense the decision made. Peter would never want for anything, having the business, his family, and his relatively stable, if not ornery, disposition. But John—who David reckoned was liable to lose at least a few wives over the years, and who one day would be too old and feeble to monetize the expeditions that enthralled him—would need help. He was a hungry ghost of a man. Never satisfied, never full.

Besides, there was a certain aesthetic soundness to the decision, which appealed to parts of

David that he had long subdued. John would use the money to bring flowers into the world, not tree stumps. In Peter's hands, the fortune would simply manifest more clearcuts, more paper, more currency. With the reaper at the door, David regarded his life's work as a pointless waste—a cancer in its own right—and not much interest to him anymore. He only wished he'd be around to see what John would do with it all.

"WHEN IT RAINS IT POURS," and "bad things come in threes" are common maxims. But why? The average individual accepts these ideas as a priori verities, without ever stopping to ponder, much less proffer an explanation for them. Nobody can account for the apparent capriciousness of the universe. One day it doesn't seem to know or care about you. The next, you find yourself subject to its unwavering adoration or unrelenting scorn.

Which particular deity John Mercer cursed or when, he did not know. Nor did he know where he stood on such cosmic questions as these. All he knew was that from the moment he heard about his father's cancer, his life had begun to spin wildly out of control, one foundational piece at a time. Sure, the inheritance was a welcome windfall. With $30 million in hand, the game of life was essentially over, and by conventional measures, John won. He could do anything he liked for the rest of his days. But what good was such freedom now that his father was gone and Peter hated him? And then there was Brooke. As his father lay dying, John had thought he would finally take her to Paris: see the Louvre, eat cheese, drink wine, get away from it all. Now, as she walked in the door of the Wallingford café to sign the divorce papers on that sunny day in May 2014, Paris was out the window, and all the money in the world didn't mean a thing. He stood up to greet her as she approached. Meant to pull out a chair for her, but forgot. She was always going on about how he could be more chivalrous once in a while. *Another failing*, he thought. *Another falling short.*

She hugged him lightly, quickly, pulled out a chair and sat down. The waiter came over, and she ordered a cranberry-orange scone and a cappuccino, which came out with a little heart drawn into the foam. She looked at the heart, wondering if she would remember this moment forever. She briefly imagined an alternate universe in which she looked up to see John crying. They would embrace, rip up the papers, and start all over again. But when she looked into his eyes, searching for some sign of emotion, he was stoic as usual. What was he thinking? She never had a clue, even now. When he broke off eye contact and began leafing through the papers, she knew it was over. And she was relieved.

Things between her and John had devolved continually over the past two years, as Lahuenco—she shuddered just to hear the name—became a bigger and bigger part of his life. His first trip had lasted a month, and that had been long enough in her mind. His second trip, two and a half. His third trip, four. She could see where this was going—not that seeing required a crystal ball, as John made it clear that eventually they would be spending half the year down there. "Expats," he said, "like a Hemingway novel," as if that was supposed to make it sound more enticing to her. She joined him for a month on his second trip. And it was true—the place was spectacular. Almost beyond belief. But so were many places back home. Brooke was, above all else, a social being. She didn't want to live halfway around the world communing with trees and granite walls, cut off from her friends and family. She didn't want to devote her life to Lahuenco. John did, and he was not one to compromise. It was that simple.

Brooke felt cruel separating from John so soon after his father's death. She hadn't planned or wanted it that way. But she had already made up her mind, and to her, time was of the essence. John would be fine, she told herself. But she wouldn't be unless she took back control of her life. She had just been accepted into the Yale School of Forestry and Environmental Studies. She hadn't even divulged to John that she had applied, knowing full well that he would never have migrated with her to the "dreaded" (as he called it) East Coast anyway. Better to make a clean break now than wait for some moment in the vague, indeterminate future.

She had insisted, much to her lawyer's chagrin, that she would accept no part of John's inheritance. For starters, she worried what people would say about her if she separated from John and cashed out so soon after David's death. But more importantly, she didn't want that life. She wanted to earn her way through the world through hard work, grit, and determination—traits she had nurtured in herself since long before she met John. And so, there was really very little to talk about. John didn't beg her to stay, and she didn't urge him to. They signed the papers, drank their coffees, paid the bill, stood up, looked at one another, shook hands, and walked away in opposite directions. It was the strangest moment of either of their lives.

John had hardly had a moment to think about the end of his marriage, preoccupied as he was with his father's death. On a strictly analytical level, he understood that he was a wreck. But emotionally, he felt constipated. He tried to cry but couldn't. He thought of Brooke, thought of his father, tried to conjure happy memories of each. Nothing seemed to animate him. He felt like Meursault in Camus's *L'Étranger*: more aware of the sun beating down on him—the end of nine long months of Pacific Northwest rain—than the subcutaneous feelings welling up within him.

Eventually the dam burst, and John was inundated with devastation. Brooke and David had been his confidants. His tethers to solid ground. Other things he couldn't (or wouldn't) put a finger on. Now, with both gone from his life, he had no one but Gary to turn to, and nothing but Lahuenco to think of to distract himself from the life unraveling before his eyes.

And yet, Lahuenco provided more than enough distraction. Back in 2013, on a rainy day in Calihue, Nahuel had explained to John that the Río Lahuenco was slated for damming by the Santiago-based hydroelectric giant Aguanergia SA.

John had laughed at first, the idea seeming absurd and reckless beyond belief. Then, seeing the seriousness in Nahuel's eyes, he realized that the situation was, in fact, quite dire. The laughability of the idea owed to how unthinkable it was. And yet, hadn't the damming of Hetch Hetchy been just as unthinkable? What river in all the world could one think of damming if one could actually think of that river? With so much at stake down south, John found it increasingly difficult to care about his own life, and the people in it, up north.

John had been dogged in his efforts to spread word of the proposed dam far and wide—public outcry having always been the only apparent way to combat the heedless machinations of extractive industries. He formed a nonprofit called Fundo Lahuenco, filed 501(c)(3) papers, and dipped into his inheritance to hire Chilean lawyers to lay out a long-term conservation strategy for the Lahuenco River and the surrounding mountains. He even put a PR team on retainer and tasked them with the job of plastering the climbing media with conservation-minded articles and images of Lahuenco. John knew at the time that this would lead to more visitors—a fact he did not relish—but compared to damming the river, he figured that to be the lesser of two evils.

But while the threat of the dam had remained amorphous and indistinct (there were no bulldozers coming up the road, no need to chain oneself to a tree) the valley had become, in the two years since John started his media campaign, quite busy. On their most recent trip there, Gary and John had been dismayed at the amount of litter in and around camp, not to mention floating in the river. The pampa itself bore the scar of fire pits and dead rectangles of grass where tents had been pitched for too long. Lahuenco was a far cry from the untouched wilderness it had been in 2011 when they first visited. It was dizzying how quickly things had changed.

THAT AUGUST IN THE PACIFIC Northwest was unusually tepid, and John and Gary took full advantage of the respite from the sweltering heat to get in as much climbing at their favorite crag—Index, an hour east of Seattle—as they could afford. And while the climbing was good and they both enjoyed themselves, Gary found John's Lahuenco tunnel vision increasingly obnoxious. Every time Gary tried to talk about Alison, Braden (who was in elementary school now and loved to read), or other things closer to home, John would change the conversation back to the problems down south. He was implacable, continually pontificating on the immense stupidity of the shortsighted assholes at Aguanergia, and speculating on how he could defeat them in some hypothetical battle to come.

They were sitting shirtless on a sunny ledge on the Upper Town Wall overlooking the Skykomish Valley when John again turned to the subject of plane tickets.

"Flights are cheap right now, Gary. We should get our tickets before they start to go up."

"Dude," Gary said, dismayed by John's single-mindedness, "it's only August."

"But we have to make plans. There's so much to do. I definitely don't want to be scrambling at the last minute to figure everything out. Let's just get the tickets now, and then we can cross that off the to-do list."

"You don't get it, man. I have a kid, a family, a job. A lot can change between now and January. I'm not just gonna buy a $1,000 plane ticket and plan my life around Lahuenco."

John couldn't understand Gary's resistance. How could he think of anything else? Convincing Gary to buy a ticket was starting to feel like pulling teeth. And last year, when Gary finally did pull the trigger, he had booked for only three weeks—barely enough time to squeeze in a handful of climbs between rainy spells. John understood that Gary cared about his family. But couldn't he see that the future of this entire valley was at stake? Sometimes there are bigger things to think about than family. Sometimes, family needs to be sacrificed for the greater good.

"Okay, what if I just buy the ticket for you?" John asked. "Would that help?"

Gary sighed and shook his head.

"John, man. Can you please just forget about Lahuenco for a minute? Look at where we are." Gary took a callused hand and swept it through the air in front of him, as if revealing the grand prize to a game show contestant. There were the mountains—Persis, Index, Baring, and Gunn—snowcapped and precipitous, framing this valley they had always loved. There was the Skykomish River, foaming and falling, cutting its way out to the coast. He picked up a pebble and tossed it into space where it clung for a moment, suspended like a star, before gravity finally took hold, and it tumbled through the air into the forest canopy below.

John, unmoved, resumed pleading. But Gary interrupted him.

"Look, John, I'll make it easy for you. I'm not going back to Lahuenco this year. Or next year. Or the year after that. I'm not going back to Lahuenco ever again. Find someone else to go with," he said, looking away. His voice quivered, and he suddenly realized that the words that were pouring out of his mouth were true, that he was emotionally through with Lahuenco and ready to move on with his life.

"But how?" John asked incredulously. "How can you turn your back on that place?"

"How can *you*?" Gary retorted, looking John squarely in the eyes. "All the articles, the photos, the social media. Look what you've done to the place. It's a zoo and getting worse. We never should have told a soul about it. We should have left it alone."

What hurt John worst was that he knew Gary was right, at least to some degree. What had once been peaceful and idyllic now looked like a modern-day Woodstock. The beautiful meadow was full to the brim with tents, the grass beneath turned to mud and dust. *Hostals* and *hospedajes* were springing up in the once-quiet town everywhere you looked. Old fishermen and beekeepers had abandoned their trades for more lucrative tourist dollars. The place was turning into another Yosemite but without the infrastructure to support it. There were no hired crews to build and maintain trails, no interpretive rangers to teach leave-no-trace principles, no cops to enforce the rules. Hell, there were no rules. It was a free for all.

John remained silent a long time, too angry to talk.

"Look at this river," he finally said. "Look at the forest. Look at your homeland. This is the valley your people come from, Gary. Look at that, and tell me how you'd feel if it was all under water and covered with idiot redneck morons on powerboats, drinking beer and blasting country music, waving American flags, or worse, the stars and bars. How would you like that?"

"*You* look," Gary said. "*You* imagine that we couldn't find a parking place, couldn't pull a permit to climb today, couldn't hear one another 'cause we were surrounded by a swarm of drones. Yeah, a dam would suck. For sure. But that's because this place is still pure. It's still real. It's not Yosemite Valley."

"No," John fired back, unable to control himself. "It's not Yosemite. But it's also not Hetch Hetchy, you dumb Indian."

John froze, and it seemed to him that time did too. He wondered—if time could freeze—if there was some way he could go one step further and put it in reverse. He yearned to reach out a hand, grab the words by the soundwaves, and pull them back into his throat. He grasped futilely; could not change anything. He tried to utter an apology, but his vocal cords would not move. He was waiting for Gary to punch him in the face and knock him off the ledge. Hoping for it. Wanting some wound to settle the score so they could agree how stupid it all was and move on. But Gary had no fire or fight in him at that moment. He was ice cold and dispassionate as he stood up and started to untie.

"Wait," John stammered, watching Gary's hands, his own body unable to move. "I'm sorry. I didn't mean that. It was a mistake."

But Gary did not wait. His fingers unworked the knot, and then, all of a sudden, he was just standing there. Infinitely loved and eminently mortal. One wrong move and he'd take the long ride hundreds of feet to his death below. John wanted to reach out and grab him, but the stance was too precarious. He feared he would accidentally knock Gary off. So he just sat there looking at him, not speaking, not even daring to breathe.

"Fuck you," Gary said. "Fuck you, and fuck Lahuenco."

And then, Gary was off the ledge and climbing. His body rose effortlessly upward, as if gravity moved momentarily in the opposite direction. John longed to feel such levity. But he was heavy and sinking. The world weighed down on his shoulders, and even with the ropes and the gear, he could not fathom continuing upward. He watched Gary ascend the final hundred feet to the top of the wall and disappear over the cliff's edge. A raven soared by, pursued by a peregrine. John sat for a long time trying to decide what to do. He thought about throwing himself backward off the ledge. But then he remembered Lahuenco, the salamanders, and the curious notion occurred to him that it wasn't his decision to make. That the universe would take him when it was ready to do so.

Finally, he went through the motions of threading the rope, rappelling, anchoring in, pulling the rope, and repeating all the way down the wall until he was back on the ground. Gary had already hiked down the trail to their packs, collected his things, and disappeared like a ghost. John packed the rope—that sacred tether of trust that exists between two climbers, two friends—into his pack. He had never felt so alone. He stood on wooden legs, plodded his way back to the car, sat in it for some time hardly able to blink, drove somewhere quiet, and passed into a deep, exhausted sleep.

HAVING LOST HIS FATHER, HIS wife, and his best friend within the span of a few months, John Mercer became thoroughly unhinged. Sorrow, guilt, and loneliness burned inside him but, like fresh lava, were soon crusted over with a hard shell of disillusioned detachment. If the world would reject John, then John would reject the world. Except, of course, for Lahuenco, which had always only been good to him. He sold his house in Bellevue and immediately purchased a modest *cabina* in Calihue, where real estate was still remarkably cheap. He donated or threw out the majority of his and Brooke's accumulated possessions—Brooke not wanting them herself, preferring to start from nothing and acquire her own things through honest labor and hard work instead.

For three months, John climbed with a reckless abandon that is still recalled today by those who were there to witness it. He free soloed routes at the edge of his abilities, legs quivering beneath him in desperation while a crowd of gawking onlookers prepared to call 911. He disappeared for days on end in the North Cascades, climbing long ridge traverses alone on marginal rock. When winter came to the Pacific Northwest, he took flight like a migratory bird south to Joshua Tree, where he again eschewed rope and partner, once dispatching one hundred ropeless pitches in a single manic morning. He seemed intent on killing himself, but death never came to take him. Gary reached out on multiple occasions, leaving plaintive messages to come back to Seattle so they could talk. But John ignored Gary's entreaties. Everywhere he went, he preached the Lahuenco gospel like a traveling salesman. "Go see the Yosemite of South America before it's too late," he said, admonishing climbers not to wait another year since Lahuenco was liable to be underwater soon. Finally, in mid-December, he flew down south.

After a fifteen-hour redeye from LAX, John laid over in the sprawling metropolis of Santiago for three days. On past trips, he had always skipped the smog-choked city, electing instead to continue straight away to the southern fjords of Patagonia. There was nothing in Santiago that interested him—just another human wasteland that must have been beautiful long ago. But he had meetings with lawyers and the director of the Servicio Nacional de Turismo. He learned that it would be possible to purchase the land and water rights to the Lahuenco watershed, though difficult. Both were held by Ernesto Ackermann—a real estate magnate and *empresario*, one of the wealthiest men in Chile, and a confidant of Chile's president, Cristobal Cárdenas. Ackermann had assiduously acquired the patchwork of parcels over the past two decades for next to nothing, his legal team offering to buy the largely unused lands for little more than the tax debts they had been accruing for years. The water rights were owned by Aguanergia—the very company planning to dam the Río Lahuenco—of which Ackermann was a primary stakeholder. While hydroelectric dams were being phased out through much of the developed world, in Chile, where mountains and rivers were ubiquitous and water rights were not a federally managed resource but a privatized commodity, hydropower was still a vibrant industry. Purchasing the land and water rights to Lahuenco could be done, John's lawyers assured him. Anything could be done. But it would cost a fortune that even John, with his sizable inheritance, did not have. And even that would be useless, unless he could convince Sr.

Ackermann to sell.

John had one more stop to make in Santiago before continuing south to Calihue. He couldn't stop thinking about that strange salamander he had been seeing up on the alpine ridges for the past few years. It didn't seem to belong there somehow. He'd tried to do some research to figure out what species it was, but salamanders in Chile were apparently a blank spot on the map. As far as he could tell, they didn't even exist. He wondered if his little salamander could be a potent conservation tool. And so, on little more than a whim, he took a bus to USACH—La Universidad de Santiago, Chile—found the biology building, and started looking for someone who might be able to help.

"*¿Salamandra? ¿Rana?*" he asked a short, plump, bespectacled man on the first floor. The man looked at him quizzically, then, intuiting his intention, directed him upstairs. Once upstairs, John asked the same questions of a grad student in jeans and a polo shirt rushing off to some unknown errand. "Álvarez," the student said midstride, pointing John down the hall. John thanked the student and walked the corridor until he saw a door that was slightly ajar.

"*¿Dónde está,*" he said when a young woman in a lab coat opened the door, pausing to type the word he was looking for on the translating app on his phone, "*el herpetólogo?*"

The woman rolled her eyes.

"*Quieres decir, la herpetóloga,*" she corrected, emphasizing the feminine pronoun.

"*Sí,*" John replied, blushing slightly before the curly haired brunette in front of him. "*¿Perdóname, dónde puedo encontrar la herpetóloga?*"

"In front of your face," the professor replied wryly in perfect English, smiling that beguiling smile that says *you poor, stupid man* in any language. "And? What do you want with her?"

John stubbornly attempted to proceed in Spanish until *la profesora*—María Josefina Álvarez—astutely pointed out that her command of his language was better than his command of hers. He was grateful to drop the charade and speak in his native tongue.

"The Valle Lahuenco, have you heard of it?"

"Of course. It's hard not to these days, as it is the new hot spot. It is so much more accessible and unregulated than the other Patagonian parks. Many of my students go there over summer vacation. Is it as beautiful as they say?"

"Yes, very much so. But it is in trouble. The river that cuts through the valley is going to be dammed. I am trying to stop it."

"They are always damming our rivers here," she said and sighed. "It is a natural"—she corrected herself—"a national tragedy. And, how do you plan to stop it from happening?"

"I'm not sure yet," John answered, musing philosophically. "We need to raise international support, attention, awareness. A massive publicity campaign, you know?"

Sra. Álvarez looked at her watch as if to say *get to the point.*

"We need some sort of…like a polar bear," John stammered.

"Well, here in Chile we have none of those. And so I wish you goo—"

"No," John cut her off. "I know. Of course. But maybe…I found this unusual salamander there in the mountains. It could be exactly…"

He trailed off when he saw she was laughing.

"You must be confused, Mr.…what was your name?"

"Mercer. Call me John."

"Mr. Mercer," she said, ignoring his request, "you are confused. In Chile salamanders are precisely as common as polar bears. You must have seen a lizard. Or maybe it was a ghost?"

She gave him a condescending grin and began to excuse herself. But John blocked the door.

"*Espera*," he said. "Wait. *Por favor.*" She sighed audibly and rolled her eyes as he took out his phone and began scrolling through photos. Suddenly his face lit up, and he put the phone in her hand.

She paused, looking closely. Her fingers worked the screen, zooming in on the photo, then back out.

"Where did you take this picture?" she asked. "What is this?"

John smirked and slowly took the phone from her hand.

"That," he said, "is your ghost."

ONE MONTH LATER, ON A beautiful summer morning, María arrived in Calihue. She still couldn't believe what John had seen, even though he swore up and down he was not lying to her. But she had been meaning to visit Lahuenco regardless, and with summer break in full swing, there was no better time. Besides, he seemed to know the place well, and he certainly looked like a mountain man. She supposed that if she went with him, he might guide her to spectacular places she would not otherwise see. It had been raining for days, but the clouds parted as if to announce her arrival, her face glowing as she inhaled deeply the sweet smells of the forest and the salty maritime bouquet of the Fiordo Coinco.

It had been less than a year since John had purchased a house in Calihue, but he looked like a regular fixture of the community when María arrived. He was seated in his front yard on cheap plastic chairs with an elderly couple who could have been anywhere between sixty and eighty years old. They were drinking maté in the custom of the region, John pouring hot water into a round gourd filled with finely chopped leaves and passing it to his guests, who sipped the tea through a metal straw until the gourd was dry and passed it back to be filled again.

"*Los vecinos*," John said, gesturing toward his neighbors and standing up to greet María in the typical Chilean fashion, with an embrace and a kiss on the cheek. The house itself was not much to look at—a few poorly insulated rooms beneath a dilapidated roof. But the garden in front was overflowing with squash, tomatoes, and greens, the drive was lined with apple trees whose spring flowers buzzed with bees, and chickens poked around curiously outside of their coop. It was not where you'd expect to find a rich man, and the smile on the rich man's face was fuller than you'd expect as well. John was home again. The hardships of the past were, for the time being, behind him.

John filled the maté gourd from the steaming thermos and handed it to María, who thanked him. Doña Isidora rolled her eyes at this, clucking, while Don Angelmo raised his bushy eyebrows at John.

"What did I do?" María asked in English, not wanting the Don and Doña to partake in the conversation. John smiled gently and told her that in the south, you do not say thank you for the maté until you are done and want no more. She rolled her eyes but smiled and put the metal straw to her lips to drink.

"*Ay, que rico,*" she said. She grabbed the straw and started to stir, which drew further gasps and exclamations from the Doña.

"What now?" María asked John, exasperated.

But Doña Isidora replied.

"No-eh toch-eh" she said, in heavily accented English, laughing.

"You don't stir with the *bombilla,*" John explained. "It gunks up the water and gets maté dust into it." Throughout Latin America, there was a generalized sense of misgiving surrounding gringos. But in the south of Chile, the feeling was even stronger when it came to plucky Santiaguinas with straight hair and fair skin, who invariably (it seemed to Calihueños) had too much money and not enough grit. The Don and Doña Contreras were more suspicious of María than the foreigner she was visiting. John, at least, had put in his time. Some time, anyway.

They finished another round of maté, the gourd getting filled and emptied quickly now that the water was beginning to cool. María declined the next round and said gracias (perhaps a touch emphatically). The neighbors also thanked John and excused themselves, leaving him and María looking across the fjord at granite-capped peaks in the distance.

"Is that Lahuenco?" María asked, pointing.

"No, no." John laughed. "Lahuenco is in the other direction, *al sur*; those are just *más cordillera*."

"And who owns that land?" she asked. He didn't know. Perhaps CONAF—La Corporación Nacional Forestal—Chile's forest service.

"Or maybe another rich Santiagan *hueón*," he said, winking at María.

"You may own a home and know how to drink maté, but you are not Chileno," she said, clearly unimpressed. "You don't know what you are dealing with. You think you can just come in here and buy all the land and make it into a gringo park?

Let me tell you something. Those Santiaguinos are not as stupid or"—she paused, searching for the word—"*sencillo*—not as simple—as you think. You have a lot to learn."

"We both do," John said, turning from the fjord to look at her. They made eye contact, then quickly looked away. John stepped into the house. María remained standing in the yard. "Well," he said, "come on in. Let's get started."

They packed bags and ate *pancito* with cheese and fresh tomatoes, slathered in Doña Contreras's homemade chimichurri and spicy ají sauce. Nahuel pulled up in the driveway a few minutes later in a beat-up pickup truck, the front seat packed with *mochileros*—backpackers—evidently catching a ride to the trailhead. Nahuel smiled broadly when he saw María step out of the door. *Que culiao*, he thought, laughing. John Mercer certainly was an ambitious gringo. First he gets a Chilean house, then a Chilean girlfriend. *What next?* Nahuel wondered.

The college-aged kids in the front seat started to file out, but John waved them off.

"*Siéntense. Siéntense*," he said, motioning for them to sit down. "*La mujer y yo montamos atrás.*" He tried to help María into the back of the pickup, but she swatted his hand like a fly, climbing up on her own.

"Even a *pelolais* knows how to get into a pick-up," she said. John took a mental note and climbed in, and they headed down the road.

At the trailhead, the backpackers each handed Nahuel a 5000-peso bill and sped off excitedly into the forest. John ribbed his friend, commenting that business must be good. Nahuel nodded slowly, but he looked concerned.

"Money good," he said. "*Pero, no todo bien.* Not all good. Look this truck. More money mean I can buy truck. But I *solo necesito* truck because road *tiene—como se dice, pavimento*. Road not dirt now. Pave. Bad for horses."

Nahuel explained that just a few years ago, before John and Gary showed up, he used to stable his animals in town and walk them the eight or so kilometers to the trailhead. Now he had to stable them at the trailhead and pay a fee to Sr. Muñoz to do so. Even Sr. Muñoz was changing. He used to be so calm, *tranquilo*. Now, all the time he was working: hawking soda and beer and empanadas, making sure people paid to park and keeping an eye on the cars, picking up litter, helping the tourist buses that were appearing at the trailhead now with increasing frequency to turn 180 degrees after dropping off their passengers in too small a space and tearing the lawn into a muddy mess.

"*Así que va*," Nahuel said. So it goes. But there was frustration and angst—something John had not seen before from Nahuel—in his eyes.

John and María made their way up the trail—the mud from the past rain spell sucking at their muck boots. The trail was in a constant state of disrepair. One path would get hopelessly rutted out, and seemingly overnight, a new one would form from hikers who had inappropriate footwear and didn't want to muddy their shoes. The tracks were as braided as a glacial river, and the braiding caused massive amounts of erosion. John, Nahuel, and some of the other local *arrieros*—horse packers like Nahuel, who brought people and goods up to the valley—had begun building elevated causeways and bridges through the worst sections, but it always felt like a game of catch-up they couldn't possibly win. John spent much of the hike cursing and shaking his head. María, meanwhile, kept stopping to marvel at bromeliads, hanging mosses, and views of the river. John sighed impatiently.

"Why are you in such a hurry?" she asked.

"There's so much to do," he said, a glazed look coming into his eyes as he stared up the trail. "So much to get done."

In another hour, they arrived at the bucolic

pampa where John and Gary had first made camp.

"Jesus Christ," John said. He had never seen so many tents in the place before.

"What did you expect?" María asked. "University let out last week. I told you, everyone is talking about Lahuenco."

There was even a tent propped up under the elaborate system of tarps and crossbeams John had constructed for his exclusive use. Food and dirty pots were sprawled out on the table he had made out of bamboo.

"*Lo siento*," he said, walking up to the occupants, "*este es mio. Tu tienes que salir.*"

"*¿Y? ¿Dónde está tu papel?*" They laughed at him.

"Where are your papers?" María translated. "If you own it, prove it."

John narrowed his eyes and told them to move or be moved. Begrudgingly, they packed their things and left.

"You didn't have to be an asshole about it," María said.

"Yes," John replied, "I did. You have to be firm with these cui—" He cut himself off.

"*Cuicos*?" María asked, finishing his thought. "I see you have already adopted the local prejudices. Very good. That will get you far when you go to Santiago to make your business deals."

That night, they pitched their tent under John's tarps. María positioned herself head to toe as far apart as possible from John, and they both slept fitfully. While María was kept up by the unfamiliarity of the hard ground beneath her and the sounds of the forest, John tossed and turned against a familiar feeling, long dormant, that was starting to throb inside of him.

IN THE MORNING, THEY CROSSED the river and began hiking up the steep path he and Gary had descended after their first climb of Cerro Salamandra. It was little more than a glorified game trail, a winding thread through a forest quilt. Vines and branches clung to their clothes and packs. Deep ruts of mud and puddles forced them to step slowly and carefully, as if navigating a minefield. The heat and humidity were extreme, and their clothes were soaked through with sweat. They finally stopped to cool off at a clearing where the creek pooled in a tantalizing swimming hole. There was a break in the trees above the pool, through which John pointed out their destination: a granite ridge high above them at the back of the valley.

"How on Earth do we get there?" María asked, seeing only impenetrably steep terrain.

"The same way the salamanders do. We climb."

They continued up the narrow passageway, at times more climbing than walking up the steep and vegetated slope. Finally they arrived at the last exposed step of rock. John pulled a rope and a harness out of his pack. He helped María put on the harness, tying one end of the rope to it and fastening the other end around his waist in a swami belt.

"What do I do?" she asked.

"Nothing," he said. "You wait for the rope to come tight, and then you climb."

"What if I fall?"

"I'll catch you."

"What if you fall?"

"I won't fall."

María rolled her eyes at John's machismo, but she was impressed in spite of herself as he deftly made his way up the steep terrain, navigating cracks and corners and marble-smooth slabs, some of which were running with snowmelt. When he got to the end of the technical climbing, he braced himself in a crevice and belayed María up in the old mountaineer's fashion, taking in slack by passing the rope behind his back. The terrain was relatively low angle, as far as rock climbing went, but it was slippery and insecure. She climbed well for a novice, but she still found herself out of breath about halfway up. She weighted the rope and hung there catching her breath.

"*Es imposible que una sala…*" she began to say, but suddenly she saw something small and squirmy climbing up a wet crack in the rock. She leaned in to look more closely. She reached out to touch it, feeling the slimy tail, and it wriggled deeper into the crack. There was no mistaking it. It was definitely a salamander.

"You put it there!" she said when she reached the top. John assured her he did not.

"But why would there be salamanders here and nowhere else in all of Chile?" she asked. He was certain he did not know.

"Maybe its ability to climb gives it some sort of evolutionary advantage," he offered.

"Bullshit," she said. "You would see them in other places. Someone brought it here. *¿Hay más?* Show me more."

John led her up the ridge, retracing his and Gary's footsteps toward the summit. They paused at every puddle, every pile of snow, every trickle of water. By the time they reached the top, they hadn't spotted a single other salamander. She was convinced her mind was playing tricks on her. Or maybe it was him. She was about to tell him as much when, looking down, she saw another one right where she was about to put her foot. She tumbled in her efforts to avoid the creature, falling to the ground. She brought her face very close to the salamander's face. It looked at her, wearing its telltale smile, and nonchalantly plodded away.

"John," she said, shaking from the excitement of her discovery, "look!"

He came over, cautiously watching where he stepped, and crouched down beside her. They looked at the salamander together.

"You promise me you are not playing a trick?"

"I promise," he said. "I didn't even know salamanders didn't exist here until you told me."

"Okay, okay." She nodded, a mystified expression plastered upon her blanching face. "I don't believe it, but I also can't deny it. But how is it possible? And what does it mean?"

She took some pictures of the salamander, then turned to snap a photo of the location where it was found. It was then that María first noticed the view.

"*Im-pres-io-nan-te*," she said, slowly drawing out each syllable as she turned a circle to take in the entire panorama. There were waterfalls, deep blue lakes, clear rivers spilled over white bedrock, granite monoliths, glaciers on long, sinuous ridges punctuated by craggy summits, and old-growth forest as far as the eye could see. The only intrusion of human civilization visible from their lofty perch was the crowded campground in the field below. An enormous condor swooped overhead, close enough that they ducked at the whoosh of its wings, and soared away into the distance.

"It's so beautiful." She gasped, tearing up at the magnificence of it all.

"No," John said. "It's the most beautiful. It's the most beautiful place in the world."

CHAPTER III

By the time John and María returned to town, two important things had transpired. First, María had already begun formulating a handful of possible theses to account for the presence of salamanders in Lahuenco. Perhaps they had arrived on the shores of the Coinco by boat as accidental passengers. Their eggs may have somehow survived a seabird's digestive tract to be later "deposited" (as she delicately put it) in the *valle*. Rare birds from throughout Mesoamerica had been kept in cages at Chaco Canyon—maybe something similar had occurred with salamanders among the ancient Patagon or the early Mapuche. She didn't know the answer, but her brain eagerly conjured possible solutions and ways to test for them. The second important thing: John and María slept together.

They spent their first day back in Calihue in relative silence, each plugging into the internet again and drinking from the stream of information like thirsty plants in a postdrought deluge, or addicts indulging in a fresh score. John spent most of his time replying to emails about Fundo Lahuenco. But he also read and reread and finally responded to a message from Brooke. She was in Connecticut now, at Yale, and apparently thriving. "I'm going to fix what five generations of Mercers have done to Pacific Northwest forests," she wrote. "You know, try to keep your brother Peter in check. Figured you'd be proud."

John realized he was, in fact, proud of Brooke. In spite of his budding feelings for María, he even felt that he had perhaps never loved Brooke more. And yet, he managed to wall off that soft spot in his heart in the peculiar way that some young men are able to, with cold logic and reasoning. Brooke—for all her intelligence and gumption—was still rigidly stuck like most gringos in the solipsistic notion that America was somehow superlative and mattered more than other places in the world. Hell, the very fact that they called the United States "America" was telling enough. (How many times had a Central or South American reminded John: "*Somos todos Americanos*"?) Furthermore, John was sure that Brooke's environmentalist aspirations and plans would be slowly digested and converted into so much excrement by Congress's constipated innards. Her hard work would amount to little more than feckless policy changes, while the American wilderness continued to go to hell in a handbasket, plowed under by one gringo dullard after another. In John's estimation, the United States was categorically fucked. Everything that could be bought or sold already had been (including the politicians), and everything pure and beautiful was already ruined by three and a half centuries of indiscretion and greed.

John kept these thoughts mostly to himself, though, breaking his long radio silence to wish Brooke luck. He almost wrote her a purely sanguine letter—a rarity for John—but ruined the ambience by suggesting that when she was finished with her schooling she might put her education to better use by coming down to Lahuenco.

Brooke read his message, smiling and shaking her head. It was pure John Mercer: earnest, honest, and unrestrained. In spite of his backhanded remark about coming to Lahuenco (as if it were *her* that had made a mistake by not doing so in the first place), she felt some warmth and tenderness to his words—something she hadn't sensed from him in years. And while she was no longer *in* love with him, she realized she still had love *for* him. She wrote back saying as much and wishing him well.

IT BEGAN RAINING AGAIN—WAVE AFTER wave of torrential cloudbursts that the locals called *chuvascos*. The weather didn't bother John and María, though, as they spent most of three days steaming up the windows of his little Calihue shack. On the final day before her flight back to Santiago, María begged John to join her. He dismissed the notion perfunctorily, explaining that he could never live in the smog-choked hustle and bustle of that sprawling metropolis. María argued (not inaccurately) that he had never tried, and so he did not know. Besides, there was lots of good climbing there in the Cajón del Maipo, so she had heard. And what was he going to do with himself when the long rainy season settled in on Lahuenco? He would be miserable, stuck inside all day with nothing to occupy his energy. He wouldn't climb for months.

But the truth was, John suddenly didn't have much interest in climbing. At least, he certainly didn't have any desire to be around climbers. The sanctimonious lot of them thought they were so much better than hikers, so much more ethical. But they were ruining Lahuenco as sure as anyone else—constructing elaborate alpine bivvies, burning all the wood in a sensitive ecosystem, and shitting right next to pristine streams. John felt a special disdain for climbers since he was one of them. Consequently, he couldn't be less attracted to the prospect of spending his time in a crowded gorge on the outskirts of Santiago. Not even the impeccable granite of Index called to him now. Climbing for him was no longer an end in and of itself. It was simply a means to his new passion, which was to see every nook and cranny of Lahuenco. For within each crevice and fold in the range, each stream and dazzling pool, each tree and lichen and patch of moss, great beauty resided. The place was abundantly alive, vivacious, fecund. And it was aggressively beautiful. Lahuenco had cast a spell on him that couldn't be broken, and he dreamed of nothing else, both day and night. What color was the lichen on that peak? Were there bonzaiesque alerce trees rooting in the cracks? Did the salamanders live only in the cirque he had shown María, or were they in other subvalleys as well? Where were the condors roosting, and how many of them were there?

John dropped María off at the airport the next day with little more than an unceremonious peck on the cheek, and for a while, they both thought whatever had sparked up between them had extinguished itself. But the rainy season was stronger than even Don Angelmo had seen before, and the trail to Lahuenco became an impassible torrent of rushing water—doubly frustrating to John as it not only barred access but was also sure to undo much of the trailwork he and Nahuel had done over the past few months. Besides, there were various pressing reasons that he needed to be in Santiago. Meetings to go to, acquaintances to make. His legal team informed him that the grassy meadow in the valley—now a thronging and lawless campground—was indeed for sale, but he would need to come to Santiago to negotiate with the owner. It was only a small piece of the puzzle that John sought—a single hectare in a 250,000 hectare wilderness—but it was a significant piece nonetheless. He knew he'd have to go to Santiago at some point. When better than the rainy season to do so?

So he booked his ticket, and by April he was back in Santiago with María. They immediately rekindled their romance. When they weren't sleeping or making love, all their talk circled around salamanders and Lahuenco. María was aflame with

Bolitoglossa chileana—as she had named the new species, owing to its snub nose and webbed feet, both characteristic of the *Bolitoglossa* genus. The presence of this new salamander brought up so many evolutionary—perhaps even anthropological—questions that she didn't know where to start. It was imperative that *B. chileana* and Lahuenco both be protected. Whatever it took.

THE OWNER OF THE IDYLLIC pampa in Valle Lahuenco where John made his basecamp was a man named Ignacio Rojas. But when John went to meet with him at a small café near the university, it was not Ignacio who showed up. John instantly recognized Ernesto Ackermann—the Santiagan businessman and hydroelectric-dam mogul—the second he walked in the door. And Sr. Ackermann—judging by his confident yet unhurried path straight to John's table—evidently recognized John as well. Sr. Ackermann was the height of decorum as he embraced John warmly, apologizing in perfect English for his late arrival.

After exchanging pleasantries, Sr. Ackermann began to explain why he was there to speak with

John instead of Sr. Rojas.

"First," he said, "it is important that you understand how Sr. Rojas came to own that pampa in Lahuenco and how I have come to own land there myself."

"Please," John said, "enlighten me."

"Gracias. So. I will try not to take too long, but there is much to tell. The valley, of course, was originally inhabited by indigenous peoples—the Mapuche—but what happened to them is the same as what happened in your own country. No? After it was taken from the Mapuche, the valley became an agricultural fundo, shared by five relatively wealthy families from Concepción."

He took a sip of water.

"Did you know, by the way, that the name *Lahuenco* is a Mapudungun word meaning 'medicinal waters'? And *Coinco* means 'water of the sand deposit,' and *Calihue* is a 'solitary place.' Well, not as solitary now that it has become so popular, thanks to your articles and photos! But I digress. Forgive me, I am an old man. It happens sometimes. I lose track of where I am going. Where was I?" He searched John for a moment with shrewd penetrating eyes, like a condor searching for carrion.

"The land," John said. "You were telling me how Sr. Rojas got the land."

"Ah, yes!" Ackermann said, suddenly smiling. "The land. The beautiful land. Well, you see, there were wars and disease. It is the same story everywhere. And in short, the land was—what is the right word? Acquired. So it goes. A sad story. A history. In my language, of course, they are the same thing: history and story. *Historia*, we call them. Anyway, at least the names the Mapuche used remain. And by the way, many Mapuche people still live in Calihue. Did you know? Some even work for my company, Aguanergia, which perhaps you have heard of during your time down south."

"Everyone down south has heard of Aguanergia," John replied. "And everyone has heard of you too. You know, Sr. Ackermann, you are not particularly well liked down there."

Sr. Ackermann smiled at him without the slightest hint of acrimony.

"Yes, well, you are not particularly well liked up here, John! So we have something in common. But please, let me continue."

Sr. Ackermann explained that after the agricultural fundo was formed, it had proven deeply unprofitable. The land had not leant itself to cattle or sheep farming, as the fundo's owners had hoped. Even timber—which would have brought a fortune, as desirable as alerce wood was—had been an impossible proposition owing to the ruggedness of the terrain. The land was an incredibly abundant but untappable resource. For close to a century, the fundo did little but accrue taxes. It was subdivided amongst the owners' heirs, then subdivided amongst the heirs' heirs, and subdivided again and again until—could he believe such a thing?—there were now more than 250 individuals who laid claim to various pieces of the massive swath of land, which was bound to the west by the Pacific, to the east by the Cordillera Andina and the Argentine border, and to the north and south by national parks.

"Our mutual friend, Sr. Rojas," Ackermann continued, finally getting to the point, "is just one of those 250. That is, he was until I purchased his parcel from him. And his land is just the latest of my many acquisitions, of which I am sure you must already know. But why am I buying up all these parcels? You see, the entire situation is a complicated mess. Let's say, for example, you desire to make this Fundo Lahuenco into a *parque nacional.* Like Yosemite. And like Yosemite, you wish to have a road—what is it called, the Tioga Road?—which traverses the park, so visitors can access the many wonders from either side. No? It is not so bad an idea. Well. If you wanted to build such a road, you would need to have many long conversations with anyone who owned land through which that road would pass. This may be hundreds of individuals, each with their own desires and ideas. You see? It would be as if you, John, had two hundred heads, each with its own brain. Now, can you imagine trying to walk from point A to point B like that? You would never get anywhere at all!

"You see, I—like you, Mr. Mercer—am a man of ideas. I see the *potencial* of this area, and I would like to realize that *potencial*. So. For the past twenty years—long before you knew that Lahuenco existed—I have been purchasing each puzzle piece one by one. The lovely pampa of Sr. Rojas is simply the latest acquisition. There are still a number of owners I am trying to track down. Word has gotten out, of course, that I—a very wealthy man—am interested in buying, and the price has gone up accordingly. But soon I will own everything, and I will have a new title drawn up with myself as the sole proprietor, and then, I can begin moving around freely and doing as I like, building roads, perhaps making a visitor center if I so choose, et cetera."

Sr. Ackermann ended his monologue smiling. He drained his glass and signaled a waiter to come refill it.

"But, Sr. Ackermann, I know exactly who you

are," John said, "and I know exactly what Aguanergia is, and I know exactly what you want to do."

The old man laughed heartily, chuckling, then coughing, then chuckling again. He waved his hand in front of his face, as if to indicate the humor was simply too much, wiped tears from his eyes, and apologized.

"Ah, Mr. Mercer, you remind me of my son! You think you know everything!"

John was not smiling, and he was beginning to chafe at Sr. Ackermann's overly genial air of diplomacy. They were adversaries, not friends.

"I know what you're going to do," John repeated. "You're going to build a dam on the Río Lahuenco and flood the entire valley. You're going to make as much money as you can off the power from that dam, and maybe as an afterthought, you'll throw up some luxury hotels along the reservoir and build docks so that rich Santiaguinos can take their boats out on the water. You may even call it a national park. Who knows. But the place won't be the same once you're done with it. You're right about one thing. I am a man of ideas. Just like you. But the ideas we have, Sr. Ackermann, are very different."

"If that is so," Sr. Ackermann said slowly and carefully, "then why would I be giving you this?"

He slid an envelope across the table, smiling sardonically as John opened it. John took out a contract, which stipulated the immediate transfer of Sr. Rojas's land to John Mercer.

Sr. Ackermann laughed and clapped as the look of surprise and confusion washed over John's face.

"You see," Sr. Ackermann said, "I have told Sr. Rojas that I would be purchasing this parcel as a gift for *you*, Mr. Mercer. All you need to do is sign the affidavit, and the land you came here to purchase is yours."

"But if I own this land," John stammered, "you'll never be able to build a dam."

"That's right!" Sr. Ackermann replied enthusiastically, inwardly chuckling at John's ignorance of Chilean law, which he had foreseen. "Like I said, John, we are not so different. I do not want there to be a dam in that beautiful valley. I want to protect it and preserve it. I have been there myself, many times over the past two decades. I have not climbed so daringly as you have," he said, winking, "but I have seen it, and I have fallen in love, just like you. Is it so hard to believe? Can you imagine anyone not falling in love with Lahuenco?"

"Then why have you purchased the water rights? Why have you been buying up all the mining claims? How come everyone believes you are going to do all these unspeakable things?"

"Because, John"—he paused while the waiter filled his glass, then thanked him graciously—"it is necessary that these things are believed. Chile is flush with national parks already. You see? She doesn't want more. I could hand the title for all of this over to *el presidente*, just as I have handed that of Sr. Rojas to you, completely *gratis*, free of charge, and do you know? He would refuse it. It is a headache he doesn't need. Now industry, energy, jobs—that he would be interested in. But that is another story. The only thing that can convince that man to preserve and protect Lahuenco the way it ought to be is public outcry. The dam is, how do you say, *un aparición*. An apparition, no? It is not real. Look around. The hydroelectric industry is on its way out. Everywhere in your home country, dams are being taken down. You are from Washington State, no? Look at the—forgive my pronunciation—the Elwha? And here in the south, they stopped the dam on the Río Baker. My own company has had numerous proposals rejected in the last few years. The hydroelectric industry is a thing of the past. Ecotourism and conservation are the industries of the future. The ghost of the dam is only there to scare people. And why is that? Well, simple! Because large numbers of scared people can be very scary. Isn't it so? Especially for politicians. If enough Chilenos—not to mention gringos and other *extranjeros*—demand that Lahuenco be protected, the president will be left no choice."

"And that's where I come in," John said, suddenly perceiving the plan.

"That's where you come in. It's like you say in the movies—good cop, bad cop. No? I am the bad cop, John. You already know this to be true. I am despised in Lahuenco. Mistrusted in Santiago. And, well, perhaps I have done certain regrettable things in my past for which I have earned my reputation. But. I am growing old, and I will only be here for so long. What I wish for now is to undo some of the environmental destruction I have caused through my enterprise. But you, John, you get to be the good cop! You will tell the people about the dam, you will raise the money, you will build the movement, you will buy the land, and you will give it to the president to preserve as a national park, to be protected in perpetuity."

"How much money will it take?"

"Fifty million US dollars."

"Fifty million!" John exclaimed. But already he was doing the math in his head. It would be possible. Even if he couldn't raise all the money, he had a massive head start with the inheritance.

"Yes, fifty million is fair. But it is not so great a price for the land."

"And what if I don't give the land to the president? What if I keep it in the hands of my foundation?"

"Oh, John," Sr. Ackermann said patronizingly, "you wouldn't do that. That would not look so good—a gringo swooping in from *el norte*, buying a bunch of land from the Chilean people, and then keeping it for himself. *Un parque privado.* No, nobody would like that. Certainly not your friends in Calihue. But," the señor said, looking at his watch and standing up to excuse himself, "I will leave that up to you! That will be your choice to make. I believe you will do the right thing. And now, if you'll excuse me, I'm afraid I have to go. I'm running late for another appointment. It was a pleasure meeting you, Sr. Mercer."

They shook hands, and Sr. Ackermann picked the contract up off the table and handed it to John.

"Think about it," he said. "The land of Sr. Rojas is yours if you want it. My business card is in there. You can let me know whenever you like."

John watched Sr. Ackermann leave, then sat back down to finish his coffee. He didn't trust Ackermann. Didn't like him. He looked at the affidavit again, searching it as if for a secret message written in disappearing ink. Something was up; he just couldn't figure out what.

Sr. Ackermann, on the other hand, felt composed and confident as his limousine driver took him home. He smiled out the window, watching university students and businessmen go mindlessly about their days, rushing from errand to errand, dimly aware of the decisions being made by powerful individuals such as himself that would ultimately shape the world they lived in.

He took out his phone and made a call to Presidente Cárdenas. Yes, he assured him, everything went according to plan.

SHOULD A YOUNG CHILD—BRADEN PORTER, say, then at the impressionable age of seven—be inquisitive enough to wonder at the question of free will versus determinism, that child would find no definitive answer on the subject forthcoming. A crackpot philosopher may assert that those who believe in free will have it, and those who don't don't. But for all their proselytizing assertiveness, no human being—neither philosopher nor neuroscientist—can say with any degree of certainty why people change or how. And yet, for all their intriguing potential ramifications, *why* and *how* are perhaps the wrong questions. There is so much more to be gleaned, instead, from the question *if*. And here, there can be no doubt. No human comes into this life knowing how to walk, talk, even control one's bladder. We learn; we change. Of that much we can be certain. But unfathomably—owing to cynicism, fatalism, laze, or some amalgamation of the three—the older we grow (perpetually accruing evidence that we do, in fact, change), the more we convince ourselves that change we cannot. Here is the most damning of all mankind's maladaptations. For in negating our potential to change, we preclude the necessity of ever having to try. Wars are waged, ecosystems plundered, entire species—critical threads in the delicate tapestry of life on Earth—are obliterated in the unthinking blink of an eye, all because we tell ourselves nothing can be done. All because we believe that change—the one constant of which we can be certain—is not possible.

So it was that when María came home that evening and asked John how the meeting had gone, he said not a word about Sr. Ackermann. Nor did he tell his lawyers about his conversation. Nor did he discuss the meeting with anyone else before signing the contract and sending it posthaste back to Sr. Ackermann. John had long since given up on involving other people in his affairs. Indeed, the chief problem with John was his belief that all humans beside himself were blithering idiots—even the ones he loved. It never occurred to him that he might be wrong or that someone else might be right. In truth, he had trouble even imagining the individual hopes, plans, and desires of other humans. He knew this about himself. And yet, because he did not believe he could change, he did not try to. When the nagging voice in the back of his head begged him to let María, the legal team, anyone at all in, he shut the voice down. It was too late for that. The cards were in his hands now. They were his alone to play.

FOR A YEAR, JOHN MERCER seemed to get his life back together. He and María became inseparable. He taught her to climb, spending weekend days at Cajón del Maipo (which turned out to be far cleaner and wilder than John had expected), and María helped John improve his command of

Santiagan Spanish—a dialect nearly as inscrutable to the rest of the Spanish-speaking world as Spanish was to the average gringo. John was gone frequently enough that they never got tired of one another, but he was there often enough to look over his affairs in Santiago and to remain in María's present and future plans.

María, meanwhile, turned the international herpetology community on its head with the paper she published on the remarkable appearance of *B. chileana*—the only salamander native to Chile. In a stuffy conference room in Santiago, mostly filled with old, overweight white men, her research was given the same treatment as all great scientific discoveries since the dawn of the age of reason—namely skepticism and denial. Attacks were made on the moral character of Profesora Álvarez herself, and her connection with the gringo philanthropist John Mercer was brought into question as white-haired heads nodded like dancing cotton swabs. There were even those—opponents of the so-called Proyecto Parque Lahuenco, which was a national news story by then—who went so far as to suggest that the salamanders were planted there by Mr. Mercer to be exploited for fundraising purposes. Most of Álvarez's peers cursorily rejected the evidence she had compiled showing significant genetic and morphological variance from its nearest geographical relative, *Bolitoglossa peruviana*, the Peruvian Climbing Salamander, which was known to range as far south as the Andean highlands of Bolivia. It wasn't solely that her peers were closed-minded; it was also the immensity of the discovery and its implications. A salamander in Chile didn't fit in with the going paradigm. Adopting it would mean a new paradigm, and almost nobody could wrap their minds around that.

With the boons of time, space, and endless work insulating John from the people in his life, he began to repair his relationships with them. He corresponded semiregularly with Brooke, who was nearing graduation and already formulating plans with the Mercer Timber Company to sell discarded slash piles and use the resultant funds to purchase carbon offsets. The circular logic made John's head spin, but he held his ordinarily cynical tongue and simply congratulated her on what he called "her worthwhile endeavor." He even patched things up, to a degree, with Peter, who had recovered from his frustration with the disbursing of the family fortune following a recent boom in Mercer Timber's stock prices.

After two years of radio silence, John finally reached out to Gary, who said simply that he had known such a day would come and that he harbored no ill will toward his old friend. Gary told John over the phone that he had stopped climbing almost altogether. He now spent his free time in the deep, dark waters of the Puget Sound, beyond the beach at Golden Gardens, spearfishing for lingcod or simply swimming in the frigid bay as long as he could before kicking back to shore. Braden, on the other hand, had become a semipermanent fixture at the climbing gym, showing a preternatural talent for the sport. He was a good boy, though strong willed and hardheaded at times. He dreamed of far-off places and asked repeatedly about Lahuenco. He had no interest in the asinine children's shows on Netflix or YouTube, which appeared to Gary to be raising the majority of Braden's peers. Instead, he was delighted by walks in the woods near home, where he collected and catalogued plant specimens. On their recent 4th of July camping trip up to Lake Serene, he suddenly became still and quiet, gazing intently at the steep and jumbled wall of Mount Index's North Norwegian Buttress. "Look how big it is," he told Alison. And then, holding out his hand as if for her to inspect it, added seriously, "And we are so small."

"He is trying to figure out his place in the universe," Gary told John. "He reminds me of you."

John invited Gary and the family to come visit him in Lahuenco, adding that Nahuel sent his regards. But Gary politely declined, citing "too busy" and "too expensive" as his chief excuses, evading the deeper misgivings that stayed his hand.

In December of 2016, following two years of preparation, Fundo Lahuenco finally launched an enormous media campaign in conjunction with *National Geographic*, which called Lahuenco "the most beautiful—and most imperiled—place on the planet" and described *B. chileana* as one of the most important vertebrates in the world to protect. John—whose photography had already garnered international recognition—published a large-format coffee-table book about the valley entitled *What We Have to Lose* and embarked on an international speaking tour, the proceeds of which all went to Fundo Lahuenco. By summer of 2017, the tour was well underway, and John found himself before a particularly generous audience in Berlin. Many high-ranking Nazi officials had defected to Chile and Argentina during the collapse of the Third Reich, and it was a popular belief among the Berliners in attendance that Sr. Ackermann's father had probably been one of them. Herr Schmidt—a wealthy environmentalist who had holdings in wind and solar farms across Europe—kicked off the evening with a speech about the importance of science and conservation in the modern era and made a seven-figure donation to Fundo Lahuenco.

John's flight from Berlin to the tour's next stop—Vancouver, Canada—took him over the polar ice cap, and looking out his window, he was overcome by a great display of aurora borealis dancing in long, surreal ribbons of green and purple. For a fleeting moment, he felt that the world was fundamentally sound, in spite of the overwhelming stupidity and greed of the human race. The actions of individuals, himself included, were of little consequence in the grand scheme of things. Humankind itself was but a blip on the geologic radar, and even if we were in an extinction crisis it was neither the first, nor would it be the last. He wondered if there was perhaps a guiding force to the unfolding of things and if the only reason we couldn't see it was because it acted behind an unseen veil—like Earth's magnetic field, which shields most of the planet from the electrically charged solar gases and particles that cause auroras. An atheist, it suddenly occurred to him that man was incredibly arrogant to suppose that, because he had science, he had any answers at all to life's deeper questions.

Man, introverted man, he thought, suddenly recalling an old Robinson Jeffers poem, *having crossed in passage and but a little with the nature of things this latter century has begot giants; but being taken up like a maniac with self-love and inward conflicts cannot manage his hybrids.* He could remember the start of the poem and the end—*who would have dreamed this infinitely little too much?* It was the middle that eluded him. Something about Actaeon, who beheld the goddess naked and was promptly devoured by his hounds.

From Vancouver, John continued south to Seattle, where he made the rounds among the business elite and climbing dirtbags alike. He secured a sizable offering from an Amazon executive, for whom the sum was so insignificant that he joked as he handed John the check: "Comes with free shipping if you're a Prime member." Gary, Alison, Braden, and Brooke conspired to surprise John at his slideshow at the Cinema Egyptian up on Capitol Hill, causing him to tear up in spite of himself when he saw them seated together in the crowd. He gave a round of hugs after the show, then bent down on one knee, dug a small quartz crystal out of his pocket, and gave it to Braden, telling him that it came from the summit of Cerro Salamandra, upon which Gary, Braden's own father, had been the first human to ever set foot. Braden's eyes filled with wonder as he grasped the stone, beaming at his father. John invited Brooke and the Porters for a bite to eat, but they declined on account of it being a school night. John walked Brooke to her car and embraced her overly long, imploring her to join him for just one cocktail. "I won't fuck you," she told him, "but I do forgive you." She kissed him on the cheek, got into an Uber, and disappeared down Pine Street. John figured that was a pretty good compromise and was relieved she had stonewalled him as he recalled María, with whom he thought he might be starting to fall in love, though he couldn't be certain yet, not owning any firm notion of what love was in the first place.

John continued south down the coast, interspersing public appearances in Portland and San Francisco with quiet sojourns in some of his favorite places—a peaceful river valley, a quiet redwood grove, a secret tide pool–laden beach. He paid a visit to Jeffers' Tor House down in Carmel and finally arrived in Los Angeles. Conservation was coming into fashion in Hollywood at that time, and the connections John made in Sin

City would ultimately lead to more than half of the $50 million that he eventually raised for Fundo Lahuenco on the tour. Much of the money came in one massive chunk from the famous actor Jeremy Lyon—a climbing dilettante—who was trying to round out his pretty boy image with some outdoorsy ruggedness.

The tour wrapped up, and John returned to Chile, spending a celebratory week with María in Santiago before beelining it for Lahuenco, where the weather was looking good. He had been up there only three days when a helicopter came swooping in over the valley, descending right in the middle of John's campground (Sr. Rojas's parcel to which John now had legitimate title). John came running out among a tornado of trash, tarps, rain flies, and other debris, signaling frantically for the pilot to shut down the rotors. The copilot hopped out and John was about to slug him in the face when he realized it was Jeremy Lyon, who had come to surprise him. John unclenched his fists and kept his hands at his sides, but he couldn't stop himself from reaming Lyon out right there in front of the whole campground, admonishing him not to be such a rich, privileged asshole.

John's lecture left a lasting impression on Lyon, and in penance, the young heartthrob decided to do something for Lahuenco. He knew just the thing—he'd record a series of films for YouTube to tell the world all about the imperiled place and send viewers to Fundo Lahuenco's webpage to give donations. He didn't tell John—he wanted it to be a surprise.

And so it was that during his stay, Lyon made secret excursions on his own (plus an entourage of fans, of course) into the wilds of the valley. He took on a whole new persona for the videos, proudly eschewing his normal designer clothes for more plebeian Patagonia threads, and pontificating at length about the pleasures and hardships of life in the jungle and the importance of protecting such wild places. The series went viral, predictably, and millions of dollars in small individual donations poured in almost overnight. John shook his head in disbelief. If Lyon wanted to do something to help, he could have quietly donated a few million dollars more of his own money, of which there was a seemingly inexhaustible supply.

Lyon's efforts, of course, coincided with a sudden surge in visitors coming to Lahuenco. The majority of them were more experienced in the art of selfies than that of backcountry travel. It wasn't long before their ineffectually buried toilet paper lined the trail like a bloom of white roses, and their single-use plastics found their way—whether through absentmindedness or pure apathy—directly into the river and out into the Coinco fjord.

Nahuel had had more than enough of the shitshow, and he spoke to John heatedly, vacillating between spitting on the ground and gesturing toward the sky. Could John not see that the place was ruined? Garbage everywhere, too many *cuicos*, too many gringos. Even the town was *cagado*. All the houses were reserved for Airbnb, and groceries and rent had climbed so high his own children could not afford to live there.

"*Conchetumare*," Nahuel hissed between his teeth, wiping sweat from his brow. "Lahuenco completely fucked, *hueón*. You so worry about the dam, you no see the flood. *¿Cachai?*"

John told Nahuel he would hire more people to pick up litter and enforce camping regulations.

"*No cachas nada*," Nahuel retorted. "You can't tell *hueones* what to do because you no own the land, *hueón*. That *cuico* Ackermann own it, and he not here. These *culiao hueones* do what they want. You tell them no camp on your land, they walk upstream and camp and *cagar* on Ackermann land. They shit and throw trash in the river just to fuck you, gringo *culiao*, and it come down the *río* to you. And then to Calihue. To me, *hueón*. You need *poli-*

cia to clean up this *disastre*. You need do something, *hueón, al tiro*."

John assured him that he would. "*Casi*," he told Nahuel. "*Estamos casi listos.*"

In fact, John was almost ready. With the last push of donations coming in from Lyon's social media debacle, Fundo Lahuenco was hovering just under $50 million. John spent the summer season between Calihue and Lahuenco, helping Nahuel to cherry-pick a team of headknockers from the town who began imposing rules they still had no legal legitimacy to enforce. He took calls and answered emails from the tiny house next to Don Angelmo and Doña Isidora, with whom he shared morning maté sessions ritualistically. He had planned to raise the final funds in Santiago, right under Ackermann's nose, showing that it was not just the will of some gringo but of the Chilean people to protect Lahuenco. The goal was so close, he could taste it. He left Calihue in early March full of optimism that he'd be purchasing Ackermann's land by the end of the month.

WHEN JOHN RETURNED TO SANTIAGO, he found María in a state of near hysteria. One of her graduate students—a bright young woman from Puerto Montt named Maite Vargas—had been studying how *B. chileana*'s webbed feet and scansorial abilities might have given it an evolutionary advantage in Lahuenco in particular, whereas in other landscapes it may not have been nearly as fruitful an adaptive strategy. It was an exciting project, and Maite showed great promise as an academic. But there was a problem. During the years since John had discovered *B. chileana*, it seemed the salamanders had become more scarce. For three seasons, Maite found them more and more difficult to locate. Not to mention her test plots and field equipment were regularly vandalized by her peers on college break, many of whom were perpetually drunk—or merely puerile, a condition equally consequential—during their extended staycations in Lahuenco. Maite had been forced to turn her scholarly attentions away from her project, pivoting to conduct a general species assessment to see if the population was indeed on the decline, and if so, why. She handed María her findings, and the data was clear. *B. chileana* was disappearing. In Maite's impassioned report, she cited a certain subset of the Chilean population—college-aged visitors who had taken up the habit of bathing and shampooing their hair directly into the pools where the salamanders spent their adolescence—as a probable contributor to the population's collapse. Moreover, increased foot traffic was causing soil erosion, and the sudden presence of human fecal matter was filling the clear water with new bacteria, both of which Maite speculated were putting environmental pressures on the salamander, which had previously been spared the incursion of the world's most destructive species—*Homo sapiens*—into their habitat.

María lashed out at John as the progenitor of the new status quo in Lahuenco, to which John reminded her that if it weren't for him, nobody would even know that *B. chileana* existed.

"And?" she asked. "What of it?"

"What of it? I'll tell you what of it. Without knowing what is there, how do you think we're supposed to protect it? If it weren't for me, the valley would probably be underwater by now."

"Which would be horrible, but would not affect the salamander, since they live in the alpine."

"Maybe not immediately, but what about when roads and *cabinas* are built and boats and jet skis fill the reservoir? Besides, the salamander isn't the only thing worth protecting. There are puma, huemul, monito del monte, a thousand rare lichens and mosses, condors, pudú, alerce, and who knows how many rare invertebrates living in the Río Lahuenco. How would they be affected by a dam?"

"All those things are endangered and beautiful, but their known range is far greater than that of *B. chileana*. They live in the parks to the north and south and other parts of the Valdivian rain forest. But the salamander is here and here alone. Nobody even knows how or why yet. And now, because of you, it's starting to look like we never will."

There was a long silence as John and María tried to settle down and breathe again. Then she continued, in calmer, more muted tones.

"You have to stop what you have started, John. You have to fix this. It's not too late, but it will be soon."

She didn't slam the bedroom door as she tended to when they fought but, rather, closed it slowly and quietly behind her. John listened to her footfalls lead down the hallway to the front door, which opened and closed behind her.

María came back in the evening, told John she knew he had good intentions, and they made up. Eventually they made love, kind of. What transpired between them was more like an awkward pantomiming—the act as empty as a blown-out eggshell. A vague fog of discontent settled over John, accompanied by an undeniable feeling of déjà vu.

BIENVENIDO
PARQUE NACIONAL
LAHUENCO

CHAPTER IV

ERNESTO ACKERMANN SAT IN THE drawing room of his Vitacura home on a plush leather chair, staring at an austere portrait of himself. He had commissioned the piece in 1998 for his fiftieth birthday. Two decades had passed since then. He had less hair on his head now and more on his ears. The skin around his cheeks and chin sagged; the eyes and forehead were creased and wrinkled. And yet, he felt he was still fifty years old. Or thirty. Surely he was not the disintegrating body he saw before him when he looked in the mirror (or even the aged man in the painting). Inside, the fire still burned brightly.

He looked at his watch. Mr. Mercer would be arriving any moment. He liked Mr. Mercer. John was ambitious and focused, just like his son,

Matías. But he found Mercer's obsession with morality banal and childish. He was glad Matías was not burdened with the same concerns. Moral people were always wondering whether they *should* do something. *Should* was a word that held no thrall over Ernesto. He had watched too many of his peers shrink from their potential energy, their calling, because they got bogged down in the tedium of *should*. It irked him to no end. Did Picasso bother with *should* when he painted the *Guernica*? Or Stravinsky when he brought Paris to its knees with the *Rite of Spring*? Or Neruda, Borges, Marquez, who made up whatever rules they desired. Should we land on the moon? Should we split the atom? Should we clone the sheep? To hell with all of that. First, find out *how*. Then we can talk about *should*.

Some people avoid *should* altogether on grounds of faith. It is not for us to decide, they say. It is the will of God. Ernesto Ackermann was not one of these people. Quite the opposite. He did not believe in God but in the supremacy of man as the sole proprietor and author of his own fate. Moreover, the repugnance he felt toward questions of morality stemmed from the diversity of opinions to be gained on any one subject at any one time, often changing over and over again as time itself moved on. The sins of our forebears are later absolved, their norms and mores later condemned. Arguments are made, discarded, and revived for and against whatever notions of right or wrong a man might conjure. Ernesto felt nothing transcendent or universal, for example, in the cases to be made for or against hydroelectric dams. But there was a certain aesthetic to the great arcing structures that appealed to him. Something about the way they resolutely imposed man's superlative will over the supposedly wild forces of nature. A well-constructed and flawlessly placed dam felt to Ackermann like a monument to the power that created it. It was the antithesis of *should*—the union of *could* with *did*.

And one day, Ackermann thought, *mankind will manifest something larger and more magnificent still.* Engineered ecosystems or planets or interstellar starships capable of sustaining life as mankind cast off into the cosmos no more or less boldly than the first Polynesians sailed headlong into the maw of the Pacific. There would be naysayers then too. And at every step of the way between now and then. The will of the people. The will of the people. To hell with the will of the people. Give them a dam—convert gravity into kilowatt hours that they use to power their everything—and they will complain. Give them a park where they can go and commune with trees and stones—they will complain. Give them nothing at all—sticks and stones and sabretooth tigers, and what will they do? They will do exactly what they have always done. Some will complain, and they won't get far. Others will invent spears, harness fire, hunt and kill and dominate their adversaries. And they will own the day.

Ernesto knew men like John. He had dealt with them again and again over the course of his long career. John went about his life the way most dimwitted people played chess: his mind never leaving his side of the board, his plans never extending beyond his own ideas. He pushed blindly through life, perpetually forgetting that the world and his opponents had plans themselves. Insofar as Sr. Ackermann had told John that he had no intention of damming the Río Lahuenco, he had told the truth. Out comes the queen. But what John hadn't realized was that the queen was collateral for a far bigger prize. Because John was so invested in his antidam agenda, he had made the mistake of thinking that Sr. Ackermann was equally passionate about his own pro-dam profligacy. Sr. Ackermann, in fact, did not care what happened to the Río Lahuenco. Sure, it was a beautiful river, and he would be sad to see it altered. But it would also be a beautiful reservoir, and he would be happy to see people recreating there each year, jobs brought to the town of Calihue, good clean energy further insulating Chile from the carbon-heavy industries of coal and gas—or worse still, nuclear (the liberals loved that one). As always, cases could be made in either direction. It was not his prerogative to bend the will of the world to his own predilections but to accurately perceive the will of the world and use it to his advantage. That was what John Mercer didn't understand. He could have the queen. It was his to keep. Because in taking it, he stepped right into Ackermann's trap.

March 2018 was unusually wet in northern Chile, and all day long, it snowed up in the cordillera. In Santiago where the weather was warmer, the snow was rain. John—ever the Washingtonian—felt right at home. As his driver wove in and out of traffic along the road to Vitacura, he thought with fascination about precipitation and watersheds. Two snowflakes, for example, could descend from the same cloud, landing only meters apart on the summit of Cerro Marmolejo, a hundred kilometers, as the condor flies, east of town.

One snowflake would melt down the west side of the mountain into the Río Maipo and eventually into the Pacific; the other would descend the eastern flanks of the peak, melting into the Río Tunuyan and passing through the long, dry Argentinean steppe before depositing itself into the Atlantic. And from there, who knows what. Two flakes of snow, born of the same cloud, could make such disparate journeys, owing not to a difference in origins but to the precipitousness of the terrain. And yet, one storm may hit the Never Summers in Colorado, another unrelated storm pummel Wyoming's Wind River Range, and through no agency or will of their own, the offspring of those two storms could end up—after long and arduous and separate journeys—quite literally bumping into one another in the Colorado River somewhere south of Moab, conjured together by the shapes of the paths that moved them and their own inexorable gravities. *Who can say what constitutes good or bad, right or wrong,* John wondered, *when such tremendous outside forces hold sway over our lives' courses?*

Ideologically, John Mercer and Ernesto Ackermann were two snowflakes careening down opposite sides of the mountain. But physically and temporally, they were the offspring of unrelated tempests hurtled together by currents neither could truly fathom, which moved them into a meeting that would change the shape of the river itself.

Ernesto entered this meeting reserved, calm, tepid. John, having finally raised the last of the fifty million upon which he and Ernesto had previously agreed, felt triumphant. Even charitable. Perhaps the señor was not such a terrible man as his reputation suggested. He was a businessman, to be certain, but that didn't make him evil. Back when he had started Aguanergia, hydro had been a wonderfully clean energy alternative. Now the industry into which he had poured his life was on the ropes, soon to be replaced by solar and wind, which would be seen as evils themselves some day in the future (the not-too-distant future, John surmised, given the horrors of lithium mining). Ernesto was an old man looking only for some final deal to tie up and give meaning to his professional life. Not a Bond villain, just a calculated businessman.

JOHN CAME IN FROM THE rain, and Ernesto took his coat, offering him tea and bringing him into the drawing room where a fire blazed in the hearth.

"John, my friend, *¿cómo estai*? How has it been for you, this past year?"

"*Hola, Ernesto. Ha sido bien.* Not bad at all. I've been pleased to see how quickly people can be galvanized to support a good cause. And you? How is your family?"

"*Estamos todos bien*, John. *Muchas gracias.* My son—I mentioned him before—he has been studying at the Harvard. He went to Yosemite for his spring break last year. He is a climber—did you know? He climbed *El Capitan*. Have you climbed it?"

"Yes, but it's been a while. In truth, I don't much care for Yosemite. Too many people, too much traffic, too much noise."

"Well, it seems Lahuenco is not far behind. But, that will be up to you, won't it?"

"Yes." John nodded proudly and confidently. "Yes it will."

They dispensed with tea and cordialities, and with little more ado, Ernesto launched into the matter for which John had come. A coffee table sat between them, and upon it he laid two manila envelopes. John looked at him quizzically.

"Go ahead; open both," Ernesto said.

"I didn't know this would be a multiple-choice test," John said nervously, trying to intuit what the old man was up to. Inside the first envelope was the title to the land and a bill of sale for $50 million, as he and Ernesto had agreed upon.

"Well, that's all that I need," John said. "Can't imagine what's in the other one."

"Oh, I'm sure you can, John. Just think about it. Think about the river."

John felt his heart fall into his stomach. The river. His face went white as he opened the second envelope. Sure enough, inside was a contract for the water rights to the Río Lahuenco. And attached to that contract was another bill of sale, this one for $30 million.

"What the hell is this?" John asked, fuming. "This is eighty. We agreed to fifty."

"Yes, John, we agreed to fifty for the land. Don't you recall our conversation? I never named a price for the water rights. Indeed, if you'd like, you can just purchase the land today. That's certainly an option. Of course, if you do, it won't be much of a purchase since the land will be underwater soon."

"What are you talking about?" John asked. "I don't understand."

"No, John," Ernesto replied, "you don't." And he laid out the situation.

When Ernesto had initially begun to purchase

the parcels of land surrounding the Río Lahuenco, he had known only that they were acquirable for incredibly cheap. They would return a profit one way or another—whether through the sale of timber; or the mining of granite, perhaps even gold, which the great mountains were rumored to contain; or through the installation of one or a series of hydroelectric dams. What he hadn't foreseen was the explosion of ecotourism, punctuated in Patagonia by the work of the gringos Douglas and Kristine Tompkins, who purchased up countless hectares of Chilean and Argentine wilderness, converted them to national parks, and then handed them turnkey over to the governments of those nations. He realized that the highest value of the land lay not in timber, kilowatts, or minerals but in the aesthetic and emotive powers it could exude over the general populace. Like tulips in Denmark in the seventeenth century, the value could be artificially inflated and manipulated through the arousal of human interest and desire.

The moment he understood this, he reached out to his friend, El Presidente Cárdenas, to sell his holdings to the government. But the president had his hands full with the generous donations of the Tompkins already.

"As I told you before," he explained to John

patiently, "the president had no interest in another national park. Supply was high; demand was low. You see? In the eyes of the president, the land was worthless. The question then became, who would esteem the land at the highest value? And this, John, was back in 2011. Precisely when you first stumbled upon Lahuenco. It wasn't long after that I saw an article about your expedition there with—what was his name? Gary Porter?—to climb Cerro Salamandra. I was curious, so I started to inquire about you with some of my *socios* in the States. I learned that you were very ambitious and belonged to a very wealthy family. And so, the gears started turning. You really helped me out of a jam! Because of *los* Tompkins, I was faced with little choice but to simply build the dam, sinking tens of millions of dollars into it and probably not seeing a return on that investment in my lifetime. But I suddenly understood that just because I couldn't sell the land to the president didn't mean I couldn't sell it to anyone. I could sell it to you!"

John didn't say a word or move a muscle. He was glaring at the old man.

"You know, John, Santiago—it is not such a big city. Well, it is huge. But in certain circles, it is not so huge. Do you understand? Your lead attorney—Sra. Ramos, no? It is a small world, after all. My own lawyer, Sr. Soto, his children and Sra. Ramos's children are schoolmates. You know how it goes, people talk, people listen. We all go to the same dinner parties. I knew what your lawyers would advise you was too much for the land. I set my price high enough to be credible but low enough not to scare you away. I gave you time and space and let you go. At times, I wondered if you'd be able to get the support you needed. I did not know about this"—he waved a hand in a circular motion, looking for the word—"this *salamandra*. That was a fascinating and unexpected twist in the plot. But it was perfect. With the *salamandra*, I knew you'd get the money. But I also knew, John, that your father left a very large sum of money to you. And of course everyone knows the accurate value of a piece of land, or body of water, is not what it is worth but what the highest bidder will pay for it. You see? And so, that is how we arrive at $80 million. Because I know that is what you will pay for it."

"But the campground," John said, thinking he had one more card up his sleeve. "I own the campground now. You sent me the title. If you build this dam, my land will be underwater. There's no way you can get away with that."

"John, John, John." Ernesto sighed, shaking his

head. "I am sorry you have come to that conclusion. I hope your lawyers did not misinform you, or did you even discuss it with them?"

John's could feel his face turning red, and the blood boiling in his ears. He had fucked up. Hugely. All of a sudden, he realized how thoroughly he had been played…how thoroughly he had screwed himself, and everything else.

"In Chile, of course, water rights supersede land rights. It is much the same as in your country, where the government can seize land to build, say, a highway. What is it called? Eminent domain? I believe that is the name for it. Well, here in Chile, if I own water rights downstream of your land rights, I can build a dam on that water and flood your land. You see? Look up the case of Endesa's Ralco dam on the Río Biobío. You may find it interesting. Certainly, I would have to pay you some fee for restitution. But, as you know, I have plenty of money. And, of course, if you bought the land, I would even have $50 million more. So the restitution fee would not be a problem."

Checkmate.

John stared down at the envelopes, cursing himself for having been so foolish. And yet, almost in the same moment, he wondered what he was really losing. The family fortune, sure. But who cared about that? Certainly not John. All that mattered was Lahuenco. He was buying a river. An ecosystem. A species. Maybe the joke was on Ernesto. Or maybe there was no joke at all. Maybe they were in this together, conspirators working toward the same eventual conclusion, unconscious teammates in a larger game. Maybe all of this, and all that was to come, was ultimately inevitable.

"Fine," John abruptly said, surprising both Ernesto and himself and reaching out his hand. "$80 million. You have a deal."

PERHAPS THE DEAL SR. ACKERMANN cut John Mercer was not a bad one in the end. After all, who can put a price on love? Various Chilean and gringo politicos even went so far as to suggest that $80 million in exchange for the massive chunk of land that eventually became Parque Nacional Lahuenco was bordering on the philanthropic. Especially coming from the astute *empresario* Sr. Ackermann. Indeed, it is almost certain that Sr. Ackermann, had he wanted to, could have held the land at ecoransom until a far larger sum was produced. But Sr. Ackermann did not want to wait. He wanted to do the deal while his friend Sr. Cárdenas was still in office.

The motivation behind that desire was more nepotistic than nefarious, as the whole point of the transaction was to create a future for Matías, who had been captivated by Lahuenco from an early age and had his own grand plans for how the land might one day be managed. After getting his master's degree at Harvard Business School, Matías had gone on to manage various aspects of Aguanergia, more interested in the practical experience of dealing in large sums of money than in the industry of hydroelectric dams—something he loathed only a little less than John did. Unlike John, Matías thought of Yosemite National Park as a clever marriage of the seemingly contradictory values of capitalism and conservation. Sure, Yosemite Valley was more Disneyland than wilderness, but funneling all the people there provided for a purer form of conservation throughout the lesser visited reaches of the park. The business model and the underpinning philosophy of Yosemite were fundamentally sound, and he could imagine no better fate for Lahuenco than to create as close to an exact replica of Yosemite as possible. Why reinvent the wheel? Was he saddened at the thought of changing the fundamental character of the valley or even losing some (supposedly) rare species of salamander? Sure. But it was for the greater good, a necessary evil to protect the rest of the ecosystem. All that Sr. Ackermann had to do to help his son achieve that goal was to convince President Cárdenas to accept the land and declare it a national park (a difficult proposition to reject when the land was given for free), and then to instate Matías as the superintendent of that park.

But to do this in a timely fashion required wresting the land from John's grasp and that meant bankrupting him. It wasn't about the money—something which Sr. Ackermann had no shortage of. If he had asked for eighty million from the start, it may have taken John too long to raise the funds, and if Sr. Cárdenas was no longer in office, it would have tanked the whole plan. On the other hand, allowing John to retain his $30 million nest egg would have enabled him to keep the lands as a private park for far too long, not only robbing Matías of his shot at superintendency but also likely establishing a management precedent far from Matías's vision. The asking price, and the transaction, were in the end totally arbitrary—a carefully constructed house of cards into which John Mercer walked utterly blind and subsequently placed the final card himself.

It was April when John became the owner of Fundo Lahuenco. The busy summer was finished, and John breathed a sigh of relief. He intended to take the long, rainy offseason as a respite from the swarm of visitors, and an opportunity to make some much-needed updates to the campground infrastructure. But there would be no rest. Lahuenco had been running beyond capacity for months, and the pit toilets and leach fields used to manage human waste were bursting at the seams. In May the biggest rain event John had ever seen hit Lahuenco, causing the river to overflow its banks. The water rose and rose until it swallowed up all the land, including the sanitation sites. When the river finally subsided, the entire campground was contaminated, with dangerously high levels of fecal coliform omnipresent. Simultaneously, a fresh batch of hikers were making their way up the valley to enjoy an unusual late-spring dry spell on the backside of the storm. Lahuenco was in the middle of an ecological disaster. Everyone knew it. Everyone saw it. There was no choice, in John's mind. There was only one thing he could do.

And so, on August 12, 2018, John Mercer relinquished ownership of what eventually became Parque Nacional Lahuenco after only six months as its custodian. One week later, on the

19th, Matías Ackermann was quietly ushered in as the park's superintendent. The sewage problem gave Ackermann the perfect excuse to shut down the park. He immediately mobilized a remediation crew to clean up the campground, and install a more sustainable sewage system. He also seized the closure as an opportunity to start building a paved road overtop the historic trail. Construction on the Ruta Lahuenco—the highway that eventually transected the park, creating an international pass between Chile and Argentina—began before the first of September.

In the aftermath, John was either adored or abhorred, depending on how proximal to the man one was. Nahuel had never been so cold, having been demoted to a far less illustrious role under the new regime. He took orders now from pencil-pushing Santiagan sycophants who had never set foot in the valley and yearned only to please whoever was immediately above them in the CONAF chain of command—a system no more or less dysfunctional than the United States' own inept Department of the Interior. John's legal team led a collective mutiny, due ostensibly to John's refusal to keep them abreast of massively important affairs, though John suspected the real reason was that the bloodthirsty vampires perceived that his financial coffers had been bled dry. Meanwhile, things with María went from bad to worse. Like the lawyers, María was beside herself with John's refusal to consult with anyone else before he made decisions. Did he really think that the land would be better in the hands of her own corrupt government? Why didn't he just put up an enormous No Trespassing sign, fundraise for another three years, and then open Lahuenco back up to tourism slowly through a tightly controlled visitation lottery system? Or just keep it closed. There was still so much to be learned about *B. chileana*, which, at this rate, wouldn't survive to the end of the decade. Why didn't he let her help him? Why didn't he let anyone help him? Why did he always have to do everything himself?

In December, John left María and Santiago for what he expected to be his final hurrah in Lahuenco. In Calihue, he embraced Don Angelmo and Doña Isidora long and hard. They were impressively antique—in their eighties now—and carried the abiding wisdom of years in the folds of their faces, the wrinkles of their eyes laughing like crows beaks more than feet. Looking at them, he thought of that old Tolstoy quote Gary used to like: "I have lived through much, and now I think I have found what is needed for happiness. A quiet secluded life in the country, with the possibility of being useful to people to whom it is easy to do good, and who are not accustomed to have it done to them; then work which one hopes may be of some use; then rest, nature, books, music, love for one's neighbor - such is my idea of happiness." He wondered if Tolstoy, Gary, his Calihueño neighbors, had had it right all along…how he, John, could have so missed life's mark.

Aside from his neighbors and a tearful reunion with Nahuel, Lahuenco brought John no happiness. His time in the valley was no better for him than a spouse's trip to the hospital to visit a partner with dementia. Lahuenco was a maddening, confusing, irrational, and often cruel shadow of its former self. The trail into the valley was choked with the black-smoke belching of heavy machinery, which ripped up the rain forest and poured hot asphalt. At the campground, treated lumber and countless cubic yards of sawdust and mulch were brought in to replace the comfortable grassy tent sites with more durable man-made platforms. A cell phone tower was being erected, erasing the final vestige of disconnection from the modern world. John hiked up the valley toward Cerro Salamandra to get away from it all but was disgusted by the omnipresence of toilet paper, people, and human feces. He used iodine tablets to treat water from the little spring near the back of the valley where he always filled his canteen—something he had never guessed he'd have to do there. On his climb up to the ridge, he dawdled looking for the peak's namesake, but saw none. He then paced the summit back and forth, slowly walking step by step like a lost ghost. When he did finally find a salamander—none the worse for wear, it appeared, in spite of the ghastly state of things below—his heart finally lifted a little. He took a picture, smiling, and thought of María.

He spent another three days of sunny weather walking the ridge that extended spinelike to the south from the summit of Cerro Salamandra. Lahuenco had been defiled, there was no doubt of that. But everywhere else, he saw untrammeled wilderness now protected in perpetuity. No dams would be built on these rivers, no trees timbered in the sprawling forests, not one mountain blasted in search of precious metals. This was the old American conservation model, tried and true. Make a sacrificial slaughter of the most beautiful place you can find, funnel the masses there, and use the collective will of the people to force the wedge between the wilderness (what remained of it anyway) and human industry. As bad—not bad, tragic—as it was, it was still better than anything else humans did with untapped ecosystems. White humans anyway. The Mapuche, he reminded himself, had managed to live here for thousands of years without disturbing or destroying the place at all. The model for true conservation was there. It was simply that modern man couldn't seem to relegate his desires to his common sense. Could not fathom eschewing the great myth of perpetual progress in favor of an older, more sustainable, way of being human.

John returned to Santiago in February, when the wave of tourists in Lahuenco became too much for him to bear, and worked hard to ingratiate himself with María again. He showed her the picture of the salamander, and they celebrated the small victory with a period of restored cordiality bordering on love. But like Lahuenco, there was something permanently altered about their relationship. A violation of trust. Or was it a revelation of the truth? A lifting of the veil. They stayed together in the way that fated couples often do, pouring themselves into their work so they had a valid excuse at the end of the day not to pour themselves into one another.

María and her student, Maite, worked tirelessly to locate and protect *B. chileana*, even making trips down to Lahuenco in the rainy season to study the furtive movements of the now depleted population. John, meanwhile, tried to salvage what remained of his nonprofit. He focused largely on Santiago, trying to convince citizens to write their congressional representatives and demand that construction on the Lahuenco road be halted and that no further projects be undertaken until a rigorous environmental-impact study could be completed, starting with a thorough examination of the effects of tourism on *B. chileana.* But what he perceived as a great defeat almost everyone else he spoke with saw as a grand victory. People didn't want to bemoan this new national park—they wanted to celebrate it. It was closer to the major city centers than the other popular Patagonian parks—enough so that a motivated (i.e., wealthy) individual could get there from Santiago on a long weekend. Parque Lahuenco was the realization of a long-anticipated Chilean dream. It was the peoples' park. The democratization of wilderness. What was a salamander compared to that?

THEN OCTOBER CAME, AND CHILE erupted into its largest bout of political strife since Pinochet's coup in 1973. A nominal (but deeply symbolic) raise in subway fares in Santiago was the straw that broke the long-suffering camel's back. Streets filled overnight with protestors, who demanded greater economic parity between the rich and the poor and a rewriting of the constitution. Any fundraising dinners and congressional meetings John had organized were peremptorily canceled, and everywhere he turned, it seemed his acquaintances had no love to give to a lizard-loving gringo, whose own government had sown the neoliberal seeds that bore the bitter fruits of Chile's current socioeconomic crisis. The people pulled inward; even María temporarily forgot about *B. chileana* as her attentions and energies turned to the quivering streets, which overflowed with police brutality and corruption. Police launched Molotov cocktails into residential buildings out of the windows of unmarked cars and incited riots and street fights. The international media fell for the ruse, blaming the violence on peaceful protestors. President Cárdenas used the farce to justify bringing in the military, who plundered, pillaged, dragged rescue personnel from the side of the wounded and dying, and other unspeakable atrocities.

When the roiling streets finally began to calm, Parque Nacional Lahuenco was set on the table as a bargaining chip in the efforts to revive some degree of civility to the war-torn country. Superintendent Matías Ackermann proposed a graduated entrance fee to Lahuenco—a program that, if successful, would later be applied throughout all Chile's national parks. The new system would charge Chileans entrance and camping fees proportional to their income—all they needed to do was bring a copy of their latest tax return. Foreigners traveling to Chile on business would automatically be slapped with the $150 USD per-vehicle entrance and $50 per-person per-night camping fees that capped off the highest income bracket. Meanwhile, low-income families and students could get in for as little as a $25 USD entrance fee, and $5 USD per person per night for camping. The new system was heralded as the first truly democratic thing to happen in the country since Pinochet.

Superintendent Ackermann's plan wasn't as innocuous as it might have seemed, for it included a provision for special lodging to keep those upper echelons of society, who paid so much more for admission, happy. This new hotel—modeled, of course, after Yosemite's Ahwahnee—would be built upon the summit of Cerro Salamandra. Meanwhile, in order to make the hotel more accessible, the technical terrain John had taken María up, where she had first seen *B. chileana*, would be blasted with dynamite into a steep and dramatic staircase with steel cables (a la Half Dome). Nahuel, who was put in charge of the whole operation, asked John via email what he thought of his legacy now. John had no response.

The icing on the cake was the helipad to be built on top of the lodge, allowing for the uber elite to arrive at the spectacular location without the slightest physical exertion. The plan, of course, was as disastrous as it was thoughtless. Even Donald Trump—the plodding idiot in chief of *Gringolandia*—hadn't built a hotel and a helicopter landing pad on top of Half Dome.

John, María, and various conservation organizations pleaded with anyone who would listen to stop the construction, which would surely annihilate the straggling survivors of *B. chileana*. But they were met with impenetrable apathy. On the other side of their efforts—countless long days and sleepless nights—John and María found that they had also exhausted whatever was left between them. The flame was extinguished. John was through with Chile, María was through with John, and they agreed to go their separate ways.

ONCE AGAIN, JOHN MERCER WENT AWOL.

He returned to the states, bought an old Chevy Astro van from a plumber in Seattle, slapped a plywood frame and a foam mattress in the back, and called it home. Curiously, he returned to climbing. Or it may be instead, climbing returned to him. For six years, he bopped around the same old haunts in the American West that he used to. Cochise and Joshua Tree in the winter, Indian Creek in the shoulder seasons, the Pacific Northwest in the summer. He was beholden to nobody. He spent most of his time on obscure free-soloing circuits of easier routes. He was not trying to die, as he once had been, he simply didn't care. He'd cast off on pitch after pitch thoroughly outside of himself, watching the body move of its own accord, wondering detachedly if this climb would be the one that got him. It never was. He didn't talk to anyone, and nobody talked to him. And that was fine. He had had his fill of humanity.

But when he closed up the van door for the evening and turned out the light, the voices around certain campfires grew suddenly quiet. And in awed whispers, one wide-eyed climber might say to another, "Dude, do you know who that is?" Everyone would look around to see who was cool and who was not. And then the coolest of the cool would inform the rest of them: "That's John Mercer."

CHAPTER V

YOU COULDN'T MISS HIM AT the crag. He wore a black leather jacket studded with metal spikes and a mohawk painted in black and red stripes. He went shirtless even in the cold (he claimed it helped to temper the body, like steel), and his whole physique rippled with sinewy muscle. He had dark skin; high, prominent cheekbones; an aquiline nose; and narrow, tapered eyes. He climbed like a prowling panther, his energy simultaneously intense, and fluid and relaxed as a tai chi master. He neither invited crowds nor rejected them. He chopped bolts he didn't like, quoted Preuss and Messner, and had a particular vendetta against the use of chalk. He could have been anything in the world he chose to be. He chose to be a climbing demigod and, at eighteen years old, was well on his way to becoming one.

John noticed him like everybody else. He had neither beef with nor interest in the kid, whom he took to be a showboat. He kept to himself, climbing his secret circuits in the early morning hours, then retreating wordlessly to his van and his books. The Hidden Valley campground was crawling with a whole "tribe"—as they called themselves—of climbers. John called them imbeciles. They loved to appropriate the spiritual values and lingo of Native Americans—but how many of them knew anything about, or did anything to give back, to those communities? How many of them even voted? Besides, he couldn't get over the so-called "vanlife" revolution. Back in his day, dirtbags subsisted off dumpster diving and lived in cramped, beater cars. Now it seemed like owning a ridiculously expensive Sprinter van was a prerequisite for calling oneself a climber. There seemed to be more and more of these vansions each week, filling parking lots like the spawn of so many concupiscent white rabbits.

Climbing today was a far cry from climbing yesterday. And yet, in spite of all the changes, Joshua Tree itself remained mostly the same. The stacks and piles of giant boulders still stood like remnants of mountains beaten down by an angry god with a cosmic billy club. The granite cast its shadow the same way every day. The cracks did not change sizes through the erosive forces of repeat traffic like those at Indian Creek. The popular routes were coated in shoe rubber and chalk, of course, but the granite was still coarse and grippy. Coyotes and chuckwallas still roamed. The blue dome of sky remained immense and intensely clear. The beauty of the desert was in its sparseness. It offered little to man, so man did little to it. *Except for climbers*, John thought pessimistically.

One clear night beneath a black firmament shot through with starlight, there was a knock on the sliding door of John's van. He opened it, and a gust of cold air rushed in. He beheld the mohawked kid and asked him what he wanted. The punk said nothing, but pulled from his shirt a crystal pendant which hung from a simple string. John looked at the stone, then looked at the punk's face. *Of course*, he thought, *of course it is him.*

"Ok," John said, "You've got my crystal. So what?"

"So I know who you are," the punk replied, "and now you know who I am." They locked unblinking eyes, communicating something silent.

"All right," John said. "You want to come in and talk?" He gestured toward the passenger seat which faced in the wrong direction for talking anyway.

"No," Braden said. "I want to climb."

John looked at the cloud of breath rising from the punk's intense visage through the chill air.

"Like, right now?"

Braden laughed, showing a wide grill of straight white teeth that seemed to glow in the moonlight. They agreed to meet at seven the next morning. Most of the "tribe" would still be sleeping off hipster-beer and drum-circle hangovers, missing the best temperatures of the day. John and Braden would have the place to themselves.

IT WAS THE FIRST TIME John had shown anyone his circuit, which was well off the beaten path. There was no comparison between them in skill—Braden could spin laps around John—and hence no competition. They were figures on a landscape. Aerial dancers on stone. John would go first; Braden would follow. A few pitches in, Braden said some select words about John's use of chalk. John grumbled but dropped the bag at the base of the next climb. They parted ways at noon.

It went on this way for weeks. The season was

closing out as the weather warmed. The Sprinter vans made their exodus back to the cities or suburbs or on to the next climbing destination. The hotter it got, the quieter it got, and the quieter it got, the more John and Braden found nourishment from the place. In the afternoons, Braden would slink off to some shadowy face and solo routes John preferred not to imagine. John would find his own shade, reading books in the hollow of some boulder and watching the shadows of the Joshua trees move across the sand like a sundial. They began eating dinners together before a modest fire of twisted mesquite: beans, rice, and cheese in tortillas charred on the flames.

Braden was mum on the subject of his parents, so John tried not to go there. But it was nearly impossible. It was 2026, so that meant Braden must be—he thought backward to his and Gary's first trip to Lahuenco in 2011. Braden had been two then. Or was it three?

"I'm eighteen," Braden told him matter-of-factly, seeming to read his thoughts. "Old enough to vote, go to jail, and die for my country. And definitely old enough to make my own damn decisions."

John didn't argue, but the next time he went into town for groceries he called up his old friend.

Gary and Alison had some notion of their son's whereabouts. Braden hadn't cut ties altogether. To John's surprise, they agreed with their son. He was his own keeper. John asked if they knew about the soloing. There was a long pause, and then Alison answered. They did. And they didn't like it. But if they asked him to stop, it would only get worse.

"What can I do?" John asked.

"Be his friend," Alison answered. "Be there for him. He worships you."

This was a nearly unfathomable fact to John, who hated himself. He nodded silently, a futile gesture from a thousand miles away. "Okay," he said. "I'll do my best." He hung up the phone not having any idea what his best might be.

In April, a heat wave sent daytime temperatures soaring into triple digits. The desert sand was too hot for bare feet, and Joshua trees shimmered in the inferno like hardened denizens of a postapocalyptic world. John and Braden were the last two fools in the park, lying on their bellies in the shade of a rock pile like fatalistic lizards. It was time to move on.

"It's getting hot here, old man," Braden said. "Why don't we head north to the valley?"

John guffawed. "The valley? I burned out on Yosemite before you were born."

"For someone who despises climbers so much, you sure let them dictate where you will and won't go. I'd take you for more of an alpha wolf. Or, what did that guy call it again? An Übermensch."

"Speak for yourself. Risking one's life for something as pointlessly quixotic as rock climbing and quoting Nietzsche doesn't make you an Übermensch. If you really want to achieve some modicum of greatness, you might start by heading back to Seattle to patch things up with your folks."

"What do you know about my parents? You think I should go back home, follow in my dad's footsteps? Screw that. My dad had a chance to do something with his life. But he threw that away for the suburbs and a nine-to-five. He could have been somebody. Like you."

Now John turned on the boy, and the result of what followed put months and many miles between them.

"Like me? Like me? And what am I? What have I accomplished in all these years? I forced away everyone who ever cared about me. I squandered my family's fortune and all my efforts on a place that has been ruined by my interventions. I singlehandedly brought a remarkable and mysterious species of salamander—one of the great ecological discoveries of the past century—to the brink and kicked it over the edge into oblivion."

"You don't know that those salamanders are all gone. They could be in another valley somewhere nobody's been to yet. It took us this long to find them in the first place. Maybe we'll find them ag—"

"No." John cut him off, his eyes cold as steel, his voice resolute and definitive. "We won't. We won't find them again. They are extinct. Done. Gone the way of the dodo. It happens every year. Happens by the thousands. It's the sixth great extinction. The bitter end of the Anthropocene. There's no bringing things back once they are gone. That's it. Over. The end."

There was a moment of silence, and Braden softened.

"Maybe Lahuenco isn't perfect now, but at least it isn't underwater," he offered, trying to console John. "And that's thanks to you."

"That's right," John said. "The Lahuenco mess is all thanks to me."

"That's not what I meant," Braden demurred. "I'm just saying, it could be worse. It could have been worse."

John's eyes narrowed, and he spoke through clenched teeth.

"When you head north, Braden, there's something I want you to do for me. Make a stop at Hetch Hetchy. Keep your eyes open. Keep your ears open. Take it all in. Then, after you've been there and seen that, go on to the valley. And when you get there, ask yourself: Which of these two places is worse? Which is the greater disaster? Take your time. Give it some thought. And when you've figured it out, you know what I want you to do?"

Braden didn't reply.

"I want you to take that silly crystal off your neck and bury it at your feet. That's where it belongs."

THE NEXT DAY, JOHN WAS gone without so much as a goodbye. He made his way up to the Cascades and across into Canada, where he disappeared into a wilderness much like Lahuenco. He wandered up alpine ridges and down densely forested valleys, unseen save for the ravens that tracked him, a sow grizzly and her cubs, and a pack of wolves. He ate salmonberries and salmon and mountain sorrel or went days at a time without food. He found a fresh deer kill and scavenged a few cuts of meat while a mountain lion crouched just out of sight, wondering bemusedly at the brazenness of this mysterious ape. The cat remained in the shadows, mistakenly attributing such reckless behavior to an abundance of confidence, owing probably to the presence of some horrible killing machine which this man, like all men, must have up his sleeve. But John was unarmed and so wayward in his loneliness that he simply didn't care who or what was watching.

In September, the rains returned to the Pacific Northwest, and John retreated once more into civilization. He checked his email for the first time in months and saw that Hotel Mercer—as it had been named—up on Cerro Salamandra was slated for a grand opening on New Year's Day. Superintendent Ackermann requested that John might come and cut the ribbon himself, seeing as the hotel was named in his honor. John was sickened though not surprised. In the years since he had donated the lands to make Lahuenco National Park, he had become something of a hero to the liberal youth of Chile—also Argentina, which now had access to the park thanks to the completion of the international highway that stretched across the cordillera. The name Mercer had become synonymous with conservation, and the story of his futile efforts to save the now extinct (or merely extirpated, as some hopefully theorized) *B. chileana* was upheld as the tragedy of a man wronged by fate. The hotel would stand sentinel over the lands Mercer had fought to protect, providing inspiration to potential future environmentalists for generations to come.

John was about to toss the email in the trash, as he had done with countless other requests for his appearance. But something shifted in him, and he began to imagine the possibility of a poetic conclusion to his life's misadventures. A plan hatched itself that day, alone in his van in Seattle as the rain beat down on the roof like a drum. He wrote back, graciously accepting the invitation and expressing his gratitude. Only he knew what he was up to.

COME NOVEMBER, JOHN WAS BACK in Indian Creek, tucked deep into Davis Canyon in a pullout among a grove of cottonwoods. He decided on a quiet Wednesday, beneath a steely sky that threatened snow, to solo the South Six-Shooter. He should not have been surprised when he mantled up onto the summit to see Braden sitting there, as stoic, matter-of-fact, and perfectly natural in that landscape as the tower itself. And yet, he was surprised. Not the least by the wave of emotion that washed over him when Braden turned around smiling. He had not realized the place the young man held in his heart. He meant to say something that matched with the feeling inside of him, but failed.

"I see you still have that silly necklace."

"I do."

"Guess you haven't figured it out yet."

"Have you?"

John paused. He had to think about it. "Yeah, I think I have."

They climbed down and made camp together. They ate tuna and beans and drank cheap beer. His tongue loosened by beer and company—both luxuries he had grown unaccustomed to—John spilled the news of his forthcoming travels.

"I'm coming with you," Braden said impulsively.

"The hell you are," John said, laughing. "Why would you want to go there anyway? I told you, the place is trashed."

"Why do you?"

"Unfinished business."

"Maybe I've got unfinished business too."

"Bullshit."

"I've got a crystal to bury."

John scoffed. He started to say something, then thought better of it. He knew what came next. They had been down this road before. He would jab, then Braden would hit back, and they would go their separate ways. He yearned for a different outcome this time. He cared about Braden. He didn't even know why, but he did. Deeply. Perhaps Braden was his last tether to civilization. *Perhaps*, he thought, *Braden is the only thing keeping me alive.*

He was silent for a bit. They ate and drank beneath a sea of stars. There was something nagging John though. Something he couldn't shake. Braden watched him open his mouth and swallow his words like a fish out of water, again and again.

"Well, what is it? You might as well spit it out."

"Nothing," John said, looking away. "Forget it."

"No, it's okay," Braden said. There was an atypical tenderness in his voice. "I'm listening. Tell me."

John sighed.

"All right," he said. "It's just this. Look at me,

Braden. I'm homeless. I'm old. I'm eating tuna and beans out of a can here in the middle of the damn desert. No wife. No kids. No friends, except maybe you. I've burned every bridge. I ruined the place I loved the most. There's a whole species that's extinct now thanks to me. A whole species! You can't even begin to imagine what that feels like… the weight of it. If I had just left Lahuenco alone, like your dad told me to, none of this would have happened. I could have just forgotten about the place and moved on. I could still be with Brooke. I could be happy."

John paused, searching the stars for the right words. Braden waited patiently.

"I know I've told you all this before, Braden. But I'm trying to teach you something. You want to come with me to Lahuenco. You want to follow in my footsteps. I can't let you. The last thing I want is for you to end up like me. You've got your whole life ahead of you. I've got nothing left to live for."

They both looked into the fire, neither one speaking. In the silence, they could hear the crackle and pop of the flames, a gentle breeze stirring the dead and dying leaves of the cottonwood trees. Suddenly Braden reached out and put his hand on John's shoulder.

"You don't have nothing to live for," Braden

said. "You're not alone."

John looked up. Made eye contact. Looked away.

"Let me come down to Lahuenco with you," Braden pleaded. "We'll go together. Climb together. We can use ropes, chalk, whatever. I don't care."

John longed to acquiesce. His heart screamed at him to smile, hug the kid, say yes, yes, a thousand times yes. But his brain wouldn't let him. Something cold and logical took over, moved his mouth, formed the word *no*. He watched it happen like a flying bird watches the land move by beneath its wings. He was out of his body, out of his head. But he knew what he was doing. What he had concluded he had to do. And he knew this was how it had to be.

"No," he said again. This time with resolution. "You can't come. Not this time."

And that was the end of the conversation. Braden didn't argue or fight back. There was no anger left in him, just consternation.

A MONTH LATER, JOHN WAS again making the long trek down to Lahuenco. He stopped in Santiago to see María, but she was busy and only had time for a quick coffee. She thought John seemed like a different person. Softer, calmer, less frenetic somehow. It was as if he actually saw her as a unique entity outside of himself for the first time. He watched her every move as she buzzed through the kitchen they once shared, pouring the coffee, sitting down at the little, round table. He couldn't stop smiling. It was unusual for him. But there was something else she couldn't quite put her finger on. A sadness behind the smile, an unmistakable feeling of melancholy. Or was it nostalgia? She tried to remember which was the more appropriate word.

"John," she finally asked, "what's up with you? You're acting strange. Is everything okay?"

"Just tired from the long flight. Don't worry about me. I'm fine."

It sounded plausible enough. She tried to see through his face, which appeared suddenly like a mask. But whatever was going on in that intense mind of his, she didn't have time for that day. John Mercer would be fine—that much she was sure of.

"All right," she said, "well, get some rest. You look like shit. I've got to run. You know where to put the key." She hugged him, put her hand against his cheek, gave him a quick kiss on the forehead, and walked away.

He watched her leave, then inhaled what remained of her presence long and slow. What a fool he was. He started to write her a letter, then thought better of it. He crumpled the page, threw it in the trash, grabbed his things, and headed back to the airport to catch the last flight down to Lahuenco.

The sun was setting over the hills as the plane touched down, and John could see pink alpenglow out the window lighting up the peaks. It was a beautiful sight. He took solace knowing that no matter how much humans screwed things up, they couldn't ruin the sunset. He caught a cab to Calihue and had the driver drop him a few blocks from his house. He carried no baggage and took his time strolling along the wharf and sandy beaches, smelling the salty air along the way.

That night he was haunted by nightmares, but each time he woke, he could remember nothing. In the morning, he strolled over to Doña Isidora and Don Angelmo's house with a thermos and maté as he had many times before. They seemed to see through him, through his plans. But they were so old that in a way, they also appeared to see through the past and the future. They accepted all, rejected nothing, were imperturbable as the mountains. They had lived through much, had seen wars and peace and the changing of the world like tides on the shore. When he bid them farewell, they said nothing. Simply held up a hand, both of them, as if they'd all be there together on Earth forever. As if time was plastic, and no matter what happened, they'd be seeing each other again soon.

John packed a bag, tidied up his house, and put his things in order. He just had one more stop to make before he hiked the trail—that is, drove the road, he suddenly recalled—up to Lahuenco. A visit he needed to pay to Nahuel.

"*Hola, Nahuel*," John said. "*Tanto tiempo.*"

Nahuel looked John up and down, embraced him, and invited him in.

"*No, hermano*," John said, excusing himself. He couldn't come in. He just had a question. Nahuel was initially offended at John's coldness. But when he heard the question, he understood. He opened his mouth to try to talk some sense into John, then changed his mind. Nahuel wasn't the type to interfere with another man's plans. John would do what John would do, and that was that.

He led John into the barn where the stabled horses blinked sleepily in the morning light. They climbed a rickety ladder into the hayloft. In the corner, Nahuel located a wooden box covered in a canvas tarp. He pulled off the tarp, releasing a cloud of dust into the shafts of light that poured through wooden slats.

"*Allí está*," Nahuel said. "*Tuyo*."

John stood there dumbly, hesitating for a moment. *There was no turning back now*, he thought. Then he thought how silly that was. He could turn back anytime he had the mind to. Anyone could. Anyone could do anything they wanted. It wasn't that he couldn't. It was that he felt he shouldn't.

"*Muchas gracias, hermano*," he said to Nahuel.

They two-manned the box downstairs, loaded it into John's car, and embraced in the driveway. Did Nahuel's eyes plea, or did they conspire? John couldn't tell. They shook hands, then John got into the driver's seat. Nahuel was walking back to the house when John opened the car door and stood up again.

"Nahuel," he called again. Nahuel stopped in his tracks but did not turn. He was the very picture of an *arriero*—face like worn leather, faded jeans, cowboy hat, and boots. "*Que le vaya bien. Muchísimas gracias. Por todo. Te quiero mucho.*"

Nahuel turned his head halfway, looking at the ground somewhere indistinct between his back and

John's feet. He paused, silent, searching for words.

"*Te quiero igual*," he said. "*Vaya con Dios*." He looked up, flashing the same toothy grin he had given John the first time they met, nearly a decade and a half ago to the day.

"Go with God," he repeated in his thickly accented and halting English, still grinning. John smiled back at him, held up a single hand in salutation, got back into the car, and drove away.

LAHUENCO WAS ALREADY ABUZZ FOR the next day's grand-opening when John arrived. Parking lots and campgrounds were at full capacity as people from all over the world poured in. Even Jeremy Lyon was there. John made his way from meeting to meeting and was eventually helicoptered up to the hotel for a rehearsal of the ribbon cutting. He was on his best behavior, schmoozing with various VIPs. After the rehearsal, while people milled around drinking champagne and eating hors d'oeuvres, he intercepted the master of ceremonies.

"Say," he said, "I was wondering if I could get a little bit of time alone with the place early tomorrow before the festivities. It's a very emotional moment for me. I don't want to lose my composure up there with everyone watching."

"Of course, Mr. Mercer," the emcee replied in perfect, accentless English. "No problem. I would feel that way too." She told him where to find the back entrance and gave him the code to open the door and dismantle the alarm system once he was in.

"Thank you," John said. "Much appreciated."

"You're very welcome, Mr. Mercer. After all, it is your hotel!"

John bowed awkwardly, thanked her again, and excused himself. He rode back down to the valley floor in the helicopter with Lyon as the sun dipped into the Coinco in the distance.

"You excited, old man?" Jeremy asked.

"I can barely contain myself," John said. Inside, his stomach churned relentlessly.

Back in the valley, John made his way to the private tent cabin that had been set up for him. He went out to the car, looked over his shoulder, and filled his pack with the contents of the box from Nahuel's barn. He went back into the house, stuffed a few extra clothing layers, a water bottle, and a lighter into the pack. He sat down in a wooden chair and stared out the cabin's only window.

The last pink light of day kissed the top of Cerro Salamandra, glinted off the pane glass windows of Hotel Mercer, and disappeared. Darkness descended on the valley. He turned out the light, listened intently to the sounds of the forest until he was sure there was nobody watching, then quietly opened the cabin door and slipped into the shadows.

AS FAR AS JOHN COULD tell, he was alone. There were various people out and about as he made his way to the Cerro Salamandra trailhead—even someone he momentarily thought looked like Braden, before deciding his mind was playing tricks on him. Whoever the doppelganger was, he hadn't paid John any mind, and neither had anyone else. When John arrived at the trailhead, he heard nothing except the beating of his own heart.

The moon was full enough that he did not need to take out his headlamp. The path was much wider now and easier to follow, with bridges and causeways over the muddy sections. At the back of the valley, the lunar light glowed on the white granite, the ancient forest casting macabre shadows on the stone staircase that had been blasted into the steep slab. There were no salamanders to be found and no climbing required. He stopped in the shadow of a giant alerce, squinting to read the plaque at its base:

Alerce
Fitzroya cupressoides

Se estima que este árbol tiene 3000 años,
más viejo que el imperio Español.
This tree is estimated to be 3000 years old,
older than the Spanish empire.

He sat down at the foot of the tree to rest, legs leaden, dead tired. The pack was killing him, it felt like it weighed a hundred pounds. He did not want to get up. He could scuttle his plans, go back to the cabin, cut the ribbon in the morning. He could forget about Lahuenco and go back home—wherever that was. He could look up Braden. Or Gary. Shit, he could pay a visit to Peter or Brooke. He could take up pottery. Learn Japanese and become a Zen poet. He could go back to Index, Canada, secret spots he knew that hadn't been ruined yet. But after a brief respite, he got up again. He felt a familiar sensation he had experienced many times while climbing—something external pushing him onward, upward, against his will or better judgment. Through uncertainty, through doubt, through fear. Always forward, never backward, let the chips fall where they may. He continued to climb.

IT WAS PAST MIDNIGHT WHEN he finally made it to the Salamandra ridge. John sloughed the onerous pack off his shoulders and placed it carefully on the ground. He looked once more down into the mostly untouched valley to the south, split down the middle by its own rushing river, which shone in the moonlight like a ribbon of quicksilver, slithering its way out to the Coinco. At one time, that too had been slated for damming. Now, as part of Parque Nacional Lahuenco, it would be protected for good. There were trails leading down into the valley from the ridge, but few people used them. For most visitors, it was enough to simply climb the arduous staircase up to Cerro Salamandra's summit and behold the expansiveness from there. Once the hotel opened, they'd be able to admire the scenery beer in hand, as if in the Alps somewhere. Next there'd be a gondola, John figured. He turned around and looked back across the Río Lahuenco at Cerro Nahuel. There were a few headlamps on the south face, which was black and backlit by the moon. The lights flickered like a constellation of blinking stars as weary climbers prepared for slumber. *Or maybe they are epicing,* John thought, remembering a handful of battles he had fought with the mountains in the course of his life. Battles the mountains had won, battles they had lost, battles yet to be decided.

He shouldered the pack again and continued up the narrow ridge to the summit. Past the spot where he and María first made love; past the spot where he and Gary slept under a single sleeping bag that starry night many years ago. The hotel was utterly alien in that environment, garish and out of place upon the slickrock. And yet, its stubborn intrusiveness almost made it picturesque, in a difficult to define way. He gave a halfhearted laugh as he read the big golden letters above the revolving front door: *Hotel Mercer*. The laugh fizzled into a defeated sigh.

He walked around back to the loading dock and found the key panel by the door. He entered the code, and the lock mechanism disengaged. He stepped inside, shut the door behind him, and turned off the alarm. He took a small paper package out of his pack, placed it on the ground, and walked into the main lobby.

The interior was impressive in the way that all gaudy, ostentatious hotels are. It was totally austere, elegant, untouchable. There were painted portraits of conquistadors and old presidents, an ornate chandelier hanging from the ceiling. He walked over to a marble bust, putting his hand upon the face of Ernesto Ackermann, dead from a heart attack two years gone by. There was a gift shop filled with tourist junk and cheap trinkets, and a large *sala* full of interactive exhibits and interpretive placards, including a life-size reproduction of a photo John had taken of Gary on the summit of Cerro Salamandra, standing triumphantly upon that vast, open space the hotel now occupied. All John could do was shake his head. He took another package out of his rucksack, placed it on the front desk, and began to walk away. Then he paused, turned around, and walked back to the desk. He grabbed the package and took it over to Sr. Ackermann's bust, placing it beside the deceased patriarch's head. He nodded approvingly and continued on.

What John had most wanted to see was the observatory, located in a broad pagoda on the upper floor of the hotel. He walked up the spiral staircase, dropping another package as he went, and ascended the last set of steps to the high point of the building.

The walls of the observatory were all glass, like a fire lookout, and the room was bathed in moonlight. There were displays with constellations painted on the walls, a taxidermied condor suspended from the ceiling with enormous wings outspread, various other exhibits and homages to celestial objects. There was a large telescope and a spinning stool at its base. He sat down and put his eye to the eyepiece. He tried for a few minutes to adjust the knobs, but couldn't quite get the picture to resolve. The cosmos remained to him as it always had been. Blurry, inscrutable, and out of reach.

Well, he thought, *I guess that's how it goes. You try your best, you fuck it all up, and in the end, the moon, the sun, the stars...they don't give a damn. Nothing ever changes. And at the same time, everything always changes. Nothing stays the same. Everything's born, then everything dies. Extinction and evolution are two sides of the same coin. Everything is pointless. All that we ever do or try to achieve—none of it matters.*

"Fuck it," he said, pushing the telescope carelessly away and taking the last package out of his bag.

He placed it next to the telescope, reading the letters on the paper again and again.

He took a book of matches out of his pocket and turned it over again and again.

He looked around the room, looked at his creased hands, took one last look at the moon, at the headlamps on Cerro Nahuel, at the Southern Cross.

He sighed reluctantly, opened the book, took out a match, and flicked it to flame.

Suddenly, he saw something move. He squinted into the inky distance, not believing his eyes. But there it was, as clear as day: a sinuous moon shadow prowling like a panther out along the ridge. He was not alone.

"Well, I'll be damned," John said. "I'll be damned."

EPILOGUE

When it comes to what happened that night up on Cerro Salamandra, the facts that are clear aren't terribly relevant, and the facts that are relevant aren't terribly clear.

In the morning, Hotel Mercer was a smoldering pile of rubble and twisted metal ringed with yellow tape and *policia*, slack-jawed dignitaries, and reporters scribbling notes. Footage from security cameras clearly showed John Mercer walking into the building at 1:32 a.m. At 2:24, he is seen exiting the building, whistling shrilly and gesticulating as he walks out of the camera frame. Over the next hour, the audio tape picked up what seems at times to be a conversation, though the sound quality is too faint and garbled to say anything definitive about who the speakers were or what was said. At 3:32, Mercer returns to the building with what appears to be a packet of dynamite. He walks backward out of sight of the camera again, unraveling a long fuse as he goes. At 3:41, we see the fuse burning toward the edge of the building. Everything goes white, then black, and the footage stops there.

That is what is known. What is not known—and a subject of great interest not just to the authorities, but also to countless people around the world who followed the story in the days and months, even years, to follow—is what became of John Mercer.

Some say he made his way by clandestine paths known only to him to the shores of the Coinco where he boarded a sloop anchored in a secret harbor and took thenceforth to the sea. There are reports that come from time to time out of the southern fjords and archipelagos of a certain ghostship—a Caleuche, as the Chilote people call it—which appears momentarily like a mirage on the horizon, then dissipates back into the Patagonian fog.

According to another story, John melted into the depths of the Valdivian rain forest that night. He'd been planning it for years—all that time alone up in the backwoods of Canada learning to hunt, fish, and gather the fruits of the forest. As this version of the story often goes, Mercer devolved into a pseudowild animal: a sort of displaced Sasquatch of the Pacific Southwest.

And there are those who claim he found his way back to Washington somehow: Changed his name, grew out his hair and a scraggly beard, took up residence in a family cottage on a remote and craggy piece of rock in the San Juan islands. That he's living there still, even now.

Depending who you talk to, you may hear any one of these tales. Or you may be regaled with a curious blend of the aforementioned legends, woven and braided as they tend to be. Like a rope or a tapestry.

THERE IS LITTLE MORE OF the story to tell. The Porters still live happily in Seattle, no longer in Beacon Hill, having moved to Ballard so that Gary could be closer to the Sound, where he still dives for lingcod among the bull kelp and the murk. Alison and Brooke remain the closest of friends. Peter is healthy, happy, and well. Mercer Timber is even slated to become carbon neutral by 2050, assuming the business (and the human race) is still around by then. Nahuel spent five years as chief ranger of Parque Nacional Lahuenco—just long enough to get a pension—before retiring and moving farther south to a secluded seaside town that won't be named.

As for *B. chileana*, the species was last sighted on December 15, 2026—16 days prior to the razing of Hotel Mercer—and is now believed to be extinct. And yet, Profesora María Álvarez and her colleague Maite Vargas continue to search for the salamander in remote and climatically similar valleys throughout the region to this day. Where *B. chileana* came from and how it happened to appear in the Lahuenco valley remains a puzzling conundrum to evolutionary biologists. Sadly, with the species no longer here to study, the mystery of *B. chileana* is one that science won't be able to solve.

If you spend much time among the granite boulders of Joshua Tree or the red sandstone of the Utah desert, chances are you'll run into Braden Porter. He's not soloing as hard or as often these days, but he still moves—still climbs—like a panther. You may meet him in darkness, when the campfire burns brightly and the flames send sparks quivering into the black blanket of night. You'll know him by the blaze, the carmine glow reflected in his face.

What you won't see is the crystal pendant that once hung around his neck. It disappeared around the time John Mercer did. You can ask Braden where it is—or where John is, for the matter, as there are those who suspect Braden knows—but you won't get anything definitive out of him.

I can tell you how he'll respond, because I've heard it said now, time and again.

"You want to know where John is, where I put the crystal?" He'll ask, a knowing look smoldering in his eyes. "Where do *you* think?"

And then he'll turn his back and walk away, leaving you alone with his reply.